The Promissory Note

Rebecca Ward

PAGEANT BOOKS

PAGEANT BOOKS
225 Park Avenue South
New York, New York 10003

PAGEANT and colophon are trademarks of the publisher

Cover artwork by Robert Sabin

Printed in the U.S.A.

First Pageant Books printing: March, 1989

10 9 8 7 6 5 4 3 2 1

"DO YOU WALTZ?"

"I expect you will now ask me to teach you how." She sighed.

"Well, will you?"

Before she could agree, Connor had slid an arm around her waist and drawn her close. Then, moving with a swift and sure grace, he swirled her into the garden.

After a few moments she stopped dancing and drew away from him. His closeness, the muted music, and the darkness left her oddly breathless. "When will you stop telling whiskers?" she demanded sternly. "To pretend that you could not dance!"

"It all depends on my partner, Rosalys."

"That is another whisker. And—and you are impertinent, sir."

His eyes shone silver in the moonlight. "I told you what to expect if you called me 'sir' again."

He put his arms around her and bent his head to hers. Her head tipped back, and her mouth rose to meet his. Their lips met.

The Promissory Note

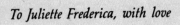

To Juliette Frederica, with love

The Promissory Note

Chapter One

"This is the outside of enough."

Gratiana, Lady Larrimer, widow of the late baronet, glared at the meager portion of toast on the silver tray before her. The butter had been spread so thin as to be almost transparent and it did not hide the fact that the bread itself was stale.

Her two daughters avoided her eyes. From her chair by the window Miss Rosalys Larrimer gazed out at a garden overgrown with weeds. Her younger sister, Miss Daphne Larrimer, sipped her weak tea delicately in a gilt chair by the fire.

"Cook must be mad! Why else would she have sent this loathsome excuse for a tea? Ring for Angus at once, Rosalys," Lady Larrimer ordered.

Now what, Rosalys wondered, had happened to make Mama fly into the boughs? Obediently she reached for the bell rope and gave it a little tug. Almost immediately, their aged butler tottered into the room.

Angus was in his eighties, tall and so lean as to almost disappear when he turned sideways. Gray hair shaded a dour Highlands face with ruddy cheeks and a nose broken, it was rumored, in a long-ago quarrel over a pretty housemaid.

"M'lady?" he quavered.

"Take this back to the kitchen and give it to the maids," Lady Larrimer commanded. "You may tell Cook that I am very displeased indeed."

"But Mama," Daphne protested, "we do not have any maids."

Dismissing Angus with a wave of her aristocratic hand, Lady Larrimer gave her younger daughter a repressive glare. "Stop bleating, Daphne, and pay attention. We have to discuss Mr. Igramme's visit."

From her chair by the window, Rosalys watched her mother apprehensively. They had gathered in the morning room for their tea because it was the least drafty in the house. It was also the prettiest. Early spring sunlight spilled through a mullioned window over chintz draperies that exactly matched the rose and cream of an elegant Chinese Chippendale daybed. Vases were bright with April daffodils, the surface of a brass Indian table was covered with curios, and fine old watercolors hung on walls papered with palest rose. The settee from which Lady Larrimer held forth had been brought at great expense from Paris.

But Rosalys knew that all this luxury was as deceptive as a stage set. Those curios with any value had long since been sold, and crocheted antimacassars hid worn spots on the settee and the damask chairs. The Larrimer sisters' twice-mended dresses spoke more truthfully of their present straitened circumstances.

Her mother's feigned anger at Cook failed to hide her nervousness. Rosalys's thoughtful dark eyes took in the pallor in her mother's long, aristocratic face, and the slight tremble in her ladyship's fine hands as she toyed with a vellum envelope. She wondered why the family solicitor's visit had caused her mama such agitation. Lady Larrimer was rarely daunted. She took all family crises—even the most inspired ones engineered by her seventeen-year-old son, Jeremy—in stride. And since Sir Henry's fatal fall while riding to hounds last spring, she had simply stiffened her spine and coped magnificently.

Eyeing the ominous envelope, Rosalys addressed her mother. "I collect you told us that Mr. Igramme had come on some trivial matter of business," she began.

"I did not tell you both the whole of it. Jeremy was still with us and I wished him to return to Oxford with an easy mind." Her ladyship sat straighter on her settee. "Igramme informs me that there is a worrisome entail."

Daphne Larrimer's amethyst eyes held a bewildered look, but Rosalys knew what an entailment signified. Though her father would never have dreamed of discussing business with his wife or daughters, she had often overheard his boasts about speculating on the Exchange. She'd also heard him roaring his frustrations when his luck changed and he lost the family's fortune.

"Is it very bad, Mama?" she prompted.

"In order to recoup his losses, your papa borrowed heavily. He hoped that his luck would change, and he would be able to pay everything off, but he died before he could do so."

"But we knew that!" Rosalys protested. "It is common knowledge that we have had to sell everything to pay his debts." Gone were the house in London, and their country house in Wynfield, along with the income from the lands. Even Sir Henry's famous stable had been sold off to raise money.

Lady Larrimer nodded. "Mr. Igramme now informs me that there was a mortgage on Larrimer House. Now that we have nothing but Larrimer House left to sell, our creditors are losing patience and are threatening to foreclose. Mr. Igramme has advised me to sell Larrimer House."

"But you cannot mean it," Rosalys protested. "We cannot sell Larrimer House!"

Lady Larrimer said nothing, only toyed with the envelope in her hand.

Daphne blinked her large, amethyst eyes. "Sell Larrimer House?" she fluttered.

"We may not have to yet." Lady Larrimer plunked the vellum envelope down on the brass table. "Read this," she commanded Rosalys.

The single sheet inside the envelope bore the

crest of the Duke of Kedwell. Rosalys raised dark eyebrows. "What is this, Mama?"

"Read it and see."

Rosalys smoothed the paper on her knee. Bold script stared up at her from the fine, creamy vellum. "It appears to be a letter from the *late* duke, the present Kedwell's father." She stopped and frowned. "Can he have been serious?"

"I vow you are being most mysterious, Rosa." Daphne jumped to her feet and rustled across the room to peer over her sister's shoulder. "Very well, I will do the reading. Hem. 'My dear Sir Henry,' etc., etc. 'I am pleased at our mutual decision to promise our children and wish to formalize the matter. Between men of honor, no solicitors are required. It is sufficient to write in my own hand that I, Reginald St. Cyr, Duke of Kedwell, agree to a betrothal between my son and your daughter.'" Daphne stopped reading to complain, "I do not understand a word of this."

"You are reading a promissory note. What was promised was a marriage contract," Lady Larrimer explained.

Rosalys folded the heavy vellum thoughtfully. "You are funning us, Mama. A marriage contract between the children of Kedwell and Larrimer? The late duke and Papa hardly had two words to say to each other. I collect that Papa always referred to his grace as 'that demmed nincompoop' —and other names that do not bear repeating."

"A trifle—a mere falling out." Lady Larrimer pursed her lips. "It was over a horse that your papa bought from Kedwell. Your papa felt that the horse was several years older than his grace had stipulated. Before their breech, however, they were thick as thieves and wanted to seal their friendship with the marriage of their children." She took back the letter, adding, "Kedwell obviously forgot about it—but I did not."

"But," Rosalys pointed out, "the present duke has a wife and four children." Not to mention, she added mentally, that he was also short, spotty, and wore a permanent scowl.

Triumph gleamed in Lady Larrimer's eyes. "There's another son."

At this Daphne raised her eyebrows so high that they almost disappeared beneath her golden fringe of curls. "I've never heard of him, Mama."

It seemed to Rosalys that her redoubtable mother hesitated for a moment. Then she said briskly, "He was the son of Kedwell's old age— by that peculiar young woman he married when his first duchess died. You remember, Rosalys, Sir Colin Briarwood's daughter, Angelica."

Rosalys couldn't repress a gurgle of laughter. "You cannot mean the Sir Colin who used to swim in the Ouse River every day of the year—in his unmentionables?"

"That will do, Rosa! It is not a subject fit for females to discuss. But yes, Sir Colin was—I shall not peel eggs with you—very odd indeed. He was fixated on matters of health. He swam daily and died at ninety of a grippe he contracted from the water. It served him right." Lady Larrimer waved her hand, dismissing Sir Colin. "After Kedwell's death, his son Connor was raised in Yorkshire, at the Briarwoods' country estate."

"He must be a perfect block." Daphne lapsed into giggles, which earned her a hard stare from her mother.

"He is nothing of the kind. He is Viscount Dracourt." A small frown pleated Lady Larrimer's forehead. "For some reason I cannot fathom, Dracourt does not care to mingle with the ton. Instead, he went off to fight with Wellington."

Daphne tossed her golden curls. "What an odd fish."

"A very *wealthy* odd fish, miss."

Rosalys had been watching her mother closely. "Mama," she protested, "you cannot mean to take this old promissory note *seriously?*"

"Why not?"

"Why *not?* By your own admission, the man is —is eccentric. He could be unbalanced. He could be a rake."

"I am persuaded that this is not the case."

"Then—but—oh, it is absurd."

"Why should it be, pray? Connor St. Cyr is a gentleman. A gentleman must abide by his word. It is a point of honor." Lady Larrimer's nostrils flared slightly as if scenting battle. "Moreover, this is what your papa wished."

"Not he! Not after he called the late duke an idiot, a loose screw and a thatch gallows—"

"He was upset at the time. Besides, it does not signify. Dracourt is not his father. And did I not mention that he was rich? He will make Daphne an excellent husband."

"Me!" Daphne gave a little scream and a jump that unsettled a Dresden shepherdess on the small brass table. "Me!" she repeated. "Mama, I will not."

"Kindly do not be a peagoose, miss," her ladyship snapped. "Do not forget that we stand to lose Larrimer House unless we can find a rich husband for you. Where will we go, pray, when we are turned out? Shall we seek charity from our cousins in Glasgow?" Both her daughters winced. "Or," she added gloomily, "perhaps you prefer that we seek refuge with my aunt, the Marchioness of Lakefield? I collect, Daphne, that when you last encountered her she compared you to a small, pink pig."

"Grandaunt Lakefield is a horrid woman. I could never bear to live with her." Daphne flounced over to her gill-backed chair and plumped down onto it. "Why me?" she demanded rebelliously. "Why not Rosa?"

Rosalys opened her mouth to speak, but her mother cut her short.

"Dracourt is close on thirty. Rosalys is twenty-four. You, Daphne, are nineteen. I grant you that it is common for an elder daughter to marry first, but in my experience," she added shrewdly, "gentlemen prefer a dewy young female to one on the shelf. Forgive me, Rosa, if I speak bluntly. We must put our best foot forward, must we not?"

There was a small silence after which her ladyship continued. "The viscount will stand by the contract, naturally, but it will help matters if he sees that his bride-to-be is a diamond of the first water. And that is another thing: He must find everything to his liking when he comes here tomorrow."

Rosalys stared. "Did you say, 'comes here tomorrow'?"

"Of course he's coming here. How else can he meet Daphne?" Lady Larrimer asked impatiently. "I wrote and invited him as soon as Igramme told me of the entail. I explained the reasons for my invitation and naturally, he accepted."

Her twice-mended cotton dress rustling a little, Rosalys got up. She clenched her small, capable hands at her sides in an effort to remain calm. "He may not offer for Daphne," she pointed out. "She has no portion, no fortune, nothing to tempt him. Mama, it is—it is humiliating."

Lady Larrimer also rose to her feet. She barely reached Rosalys's shoulder, but her determination made her seem much taller. "It would be far more humiliating to be turned out of Larrimer House. Fortunately, there is no need. The late duke gave his word. I have his promissory note." She wheeled on Daphne, who was shaking her head mutinously. "And you, miss, consider the fact that the man is rich. Consider that he is a viscount. Now, consider the alternative."

Daphne opened her rosy mouth to protest, then closed it with a pop.

Lady Larrimer nodded as if well satisfied. "I leave all the arrangements to you, Rosa. You know what must be done. The viscount must be entertained royally while he is with us."

About to utter further protest, Rosalys met her mother's eyes. She was surprised to see the entreaty in those gray depths. In spite of her imperious words, Rosalys realized, the family was in dire straits. If they lost Larrimer House, there was truly nowhere to go.

Instead of weeping and wringing her hands as most women would have done, her ladyship was fighting back with the only weapon she had left: a beautiful and marriageable daughter. Rosalys felt a rush of sympathy for her. Impulsively, she reached out and caught the older woman's hand in both her own. "Mama," she said gently, "you cannot force the viscount to marry Daphne if he does not want to do so. You do know that, don't you?"

"Stuff and nonsense, miss. Where is the problem, pray? Dracourt will be getting a pretty wife, a good name, and a bloodline that is at least as good as his own. Better, if one recalls Sir Colin— which one would rather not do." Her voice rang forth like a bugle sounding the cavalry charge. "If the man thinks he can slither out of his obligations—well, let him try!"

Rosalys let go of her mother's hand. She no longer felt sorry for her. She reserved her sympathy for Connor St. Cyr, Viscount Dracourt.

Chapter Two

Concealed in a plain black cloak and camouflaged by a shabby bonnet that had belonged to a former housemaid, Rosalys slipped through the side gate of Larrimer House and walked rapidly up the road. On her arm she carried a large, empty market basket. There were only a few hours left until sundown, and speed was of the essence. She needed to get to the village, complete her errand, and be back before she was missed.

So far, she had been lucky. Though the Larrimers' two elderly servants had sharp eyes, they were occupied elsewhere. Angus was busy preparing a room for their guest and Cook, on the verge of a nervous collapse over the viscount's imminent arrival, was searching the hencoop for eggs.

Her mother and sister were also busy. On her ladyship's orders, Daphne was attending to the gown she would wear tomorrow night. Lady Larrimer was resting—or, at least, Rosalys hoped so. If her mother learned that a Larrimer had so forgot her breeding as to dicker with the tradesmen, she would surely have spasms.

Could she dicker successfully? Rosalys closed her hand more firmly around the small velvet case she carried, which contained her grandmama's pearl earrings, the last link to a carefree life that had disappeared years ago. Though the family had already parted with most of its jew-

11

elry—Angus had made trips to London for the purpose of converting gems and gewgaws into fuel and meat—she had held her grandmama's ear-bobs back. They weren't worth much, really, except in sentimental value.

Rosalys sighed. You could not serve sentimental value up with a sauce and expect the viscount to eat it.

Lord Dracourt was arriving tomorrow. Like it or not, that was one fact. Another inescapable fact was that there wasn't a chop or a cutlet in Larrimer House. There was, Cook had lamented, nothing except leftover mutton stew. "And no gentleman as is a duke's son is going to be satisfied wi' a plate o' stew," she had added. "There's nofink to feed a gentleman of quality in this 'ere house, Miss Rosa. What'll 'e think of us?"

Into Rosalys's mind popped an image of a stout, dour-faced gentleman. "Went out to Dorset last week," she could hear the viscount drawling to his sniggering friends. "Old Lady Larrimer invited me down—some demmed foolishness about a letter from the pater. Fed me a ghastly stew and stale bread, give you my word. Nearly choked."

Rosalys winced. "What a mare's nest," she muttered, then looked self-consciously about her. The meadow she was passing was deserted, and so were the hedged farms and the pastureland that sloped toward the Stour River. Apart from a few prowling, hungry-eyed cats, there was no one on the road. But the village proper was an-

other matter; there were several women, baskets
over their arms, walking in and out of the shops.

The homely village inn, the Royal George, was
also bustling with business. The London Coach
had just arrived as well as a sportive curricle
drawn by a pair of spanking grays. Rosalys eyed
the horses appreciatively, held back a sigh for Sir
Henry's once enviable stable, and tucked her chin
into the concealing folds of her black cloak as she
hurried past the inn.

Then, as if accustomed to such activities, she
stepped smartly into Jason's Butcher Shop. The
smell of fresh blood assailed her, but Rosalys was
too preoccupied to feel revulsion. This was no
time for missish sensibilities, and besides, there
was the burning question: Beef or mutton?

Fortunately, Jason was waiting on another cus-
tomer, so she could take a few moments to look
around his shop. Most highborn ladies would no
doubt have felt faint at the sight of so much raw
meat, but months of helping Cook in the kitchen
had taught Rosalys to view Jason's offerings with
a practical eye. The beef, she decided, looked far
superior to the mutton, and those chops would
serve to take the edge off the most ferocious male
appetite.

She smiled as Jason came around to wait on
her. "Give ye good day, ma'am—" the butcher
began, then broke off. "Good heavens, Miss
Lar—"

"Good day, Jason," Rosalys said briskly. "I
need your help as we are entertaining a special
guest." The butcher's mouth was beginning to

screw up, so she hastened to add, "I collect that we have not paid our latest bill."

Jason swallowed hard and stared at a point over Rosalys's left shoulder. His muttonchop whiskers bristled in agitation. "No, ma'am. And the fact of the matter, ma'am, is—"

He broke off as Rosalys placed a pair of very small pearl earrings on the counter. Her voice was steady as she said, "Please hold these as collateral 'til we can pay our bill. Now, as to my order—"

Half an hour later, Rosalys left Jason's with a heavy basket. In contrast, her heart was light. She could visualize Cook's astonished face and the pleasure with which she would begin to prepare a feast. They had not seen such good food in a long while, Rosalys thought. Really, it was true that even an ill wind blew somebody some good.

"Hel-lo, my lovely!"

The slurred male voice assaulted her as she passed the Royal George. Rosalys had not the time to turn her head before beefy arms clamped around her waist. "Give us a kiss," the voice continued. "Li'l kiss won't hurt you."

Rosalys struggled to free herself but was instead turned around to face a stout young man. He was dressed to the nines in an ankle-length drab coat with several capes, a Guthrie's waistcoat, buff-colored riding breeches, and glossy boots. Under one arm was tucked a gold-knobbed cane. His high, starched collar and cravat in the *trône d'amour* style almost eclipsed a face made florid by too much drink.

"You are foxed, sir," Rosalys exclaimed. "Let me go at once."

"High in the instep for a housemaid, ain't she?" the foppish gentleman demanded. A gallery of male observers who had collected around the steps of the inn agreed loudly. All of the men were grinning at the scene, and Rosalys's indignation gave way to fear that she might be recognized.

"Unhand me immediately," she hissed.

"Think you're above a bit of cuddle, do you?"

He tried to pull her forward into his arms, but Rosalys kicked him smartly in the shins. He gave a yelp of astonished pain and loosened her arms so that she could hit him with her basket.

It was a mistake; the capon flew one way, the beef and chops another. Rosalys heard the joyous bark of village dogs as they gave chase.

"Oh, confound you, let me go," she exclaimed in very real anguish.

The florid face of the man who held her had become ugly with anger. "Dooce take it, my gel—"

"Now, then. Can't you see that the lady's not willing?" a deep voice asked.

Rosalys had an impression of height and breadth of shoulder an instant before the florid gentleman was plucked away from her.

"Demmed inteferin' jackanapes—"

Rosalys heard the dandified drunk swearing loudly as her rescuer sent him staggering backward, but she paid him no heed. She was much too busy trying to rescue her meat.

Two dogs had gotten hold of the capon. They were munching on it blissfully, and she had to beat them away with her basket. The reclaimed capon looked so sorry a sight that she nearly wept, but the chops and beef were safe. She was piling everything back into her basket when she heard the drunken man's snarl.

"Whoever you are, you will be sorry for this. 'Pon rep, I'll teach you to mix into the business of your betters."

"That depends on the business—and my betters."

Rosalys looked over her shoulder. Her rescuer was standing nearby with his arms folded across his chest. True to her first, fleeting impression, he was a tall man, and powerfully built. Straight of back, broad of shoulder, he carried his strong frame like an athlete, and he held his fair head proudly.

But here all similarity to quality ended. Her rescuer wore no hat or coat. He was in shirt-sleeves, and his breeches and boots were splashed with mud. He must be a groom, Rosalys decided, but since when had a groom dared to attack a gentleman in defense of a supposed servant girl?

"You will have a lesson you will not forget," the angry dandy said with a snarl. "Your master will hear from me."

The big man laughed. "Well, you're welcome to talk to him. Ah, *would* you?"

The foxed gentleman had lunged forward, flailing with his cane. Her rescuer moved so quickly that his big body seemed to blur. Catching the

cane, he spun it with apparent ease. The fop staggered backward, teetered for a moment on the
heels of his boots, then plopped on his backside
into the mud.

"Was that the lesson you had in mind?" the big
man wanted to know.

Amid shouts of appreciative laughter from the
gallery of onlookers, he turned to Rosalys. "Are
you all right, lass?" he asked.

He sounded as if he really cared. His Yorkshire
accent gave his speech both ease and friendliness.
Rosalys looked up into a pair of smiling, bright
blue eyes and saw humor and concern reflected
there.

"Are you all right?" he repeated.

"Yes. Thank you very much." Then she added
anxiously, "But you could be in the suds for
helping me. That man you knocked down will be
sure to make trouble for you. Perhaps he will
even have you—"

"Sacked?" he supplied. "Don't you worry
about that."

He was obviously not worried. And though he
smiled, there was something in the set of his
mouth and chin that told her that here was a
man who would brook no nonsense. His strong-
featured face was burned nut brown, and he
wore his shabby clothes with ease. He certainly
was no ordinary groom, Rosalys thought.

"Collected everything you had in the basket?"
he asked. She nodded, and he reached out and
adjusted the cloak around her shoulders. In spite
of the largeness of his hands, his touch was gen-

tle. Somehow, it conveyed a feeling of safety. "Best be going, then, before another sap-skulled park-saunterer thinks you're too pretty for your own good," he advised.

By now the furious dandy's shouts and threats had drawn a large crowd. At any moment she would be recognized—and she couldn't afford to have her identity known under such circumstances. But though Rosalys desperately wanted to be gone, she hesitated; it seemed cowardly to leave her rescuer in such a situation.

As if reading her thoughts, he grinned. "Go on with you, lass," he reassured her. "I can take care of myself."

Because he obviously could, Rosalys hurried away, and as the sound of male voices faded behind her, she turned her thoughts to grappling with the difficult problem at hand.

How, she asked herself, were they going to serve the capon so that the dogs' teeth marks did not show?

" 'Ere, now. What's the matter with this chicken?" Cook demanded. "You said as that Jason's boy brought the meat, Miss Rosa. I'm not taking any capon as looks like this. I'm sending it back."

"Do not do that," Rosalys began, then sneezed. The cavernous kitchen was as cold as charity. "There is no time," she added hastily as Cook's face took on a look of stern suspicion. "Can you not just cut it up into a pie?"

"What I does with this 'ere fowl isn't the

point," Cook lectured. "Miss Rosa, you went out yourself, didn't you? To the butcher an' all? When you knows as well as I does that a lady is not supposed to go nowhere without 'er abigail?"

"I do not have an abigail," Rosalys pointed out.

Cook folded stout arms across her expanse of starched, white apron and rocked back on her heels. "More reason for staying at 'ome. I could 'ave gone, or Angus."

Rosalys forbore to explain that Jason would not have extended credit to either Angus or Cook, not on the flimsy collateral of those ear-bobs. It was something she had had to do herself, but Cook would not accept that. The woman was a martinet about manners and the Family Honor —and she practiced what she preached. Though there were no servants besides herself and Angus, Cook kept her bare kitchen scrubbed to an inch of its life.

"Well, the meat is here, anyway," Rosalys said peaceably, "and none too soon. You must serve a great deal of food, Cook, dear. The viscount has been a soldier and is probably used to stale bread and moldy cheese. He is bound to be starving."

Cook snorted. "That's all you knows," she scoffed. "Horficers eats splendid, they does. My poor, dead sister's boy, Tom, 'e went for a soldier before 'e got 'isself wounded, and 'e told me as the horficers sat down to their h'afternoon tea each day. With buttered crumpets," she added as an afterthought, "and jam."

I should have thought to buy some jam, Rosalys thought. Aloud she said, "Well, serve the best meal you can. Now, I must see the room Angus has made ready for our guest."

She found the old butler polishing the brass andirons in the main dining room. "I have readied the West Room for his lordship, ma'am," he rasped.

"For heaven's sake, why? That's the coldest room in the house. I will move his bedding to the Blue Room at once."

"Thank you, Miss Rosa, but I can manage by myself." The burr in Angus's voice grew more apparent as he added, "But the Blue Room ceiling has a wee leak, ma'am."

"The sky is quite blue. There may not be rain for days. And the Blue Room is much more suitable, Angus."

"Vur-ry well, ma'am."

"And *I* will make up the bed. You have quite enough to do as it is."

Angus sighed. It wasn't for him to criticize the gentry, he thought dourly, but it was a shame that her ladyship kept heaping responsibilities on Miss Rosa's young shoulders.

To his mind she was sadly put upon. He and Cook had many times deplored the fact that the late master's reversals had come during Miss Rosa's first and only Season in London. She hadn't even had a chance to make a good match. When Sir Henry's losses had become known, the gentlemen who had been courting the now penniless deb had taken to their heels.

Young cabbage heads, Angus thought balefully. Perhaps it would have helped if Miss Rosa were a beauty in the fashionable sense—gold and cream sugar like Miss Daphne—but she was tall for a woman and had inherited her father's dark hair and fine, high cheekbones that gave her face too much character for prettiness. And then there were those long-lashed brown eyes, which were often disconcertingly direct.

They were honest now as she looked about her. "The viscount will find this a shabby place, will he not, Angus?" she sighed.

Angus's sloping shoulders drooped in his rusty black coat. It was true. The dining room was dusty, the heavy furniture scratched and marred. The Turkish carpet had a threadbare look. "I do not know what to say, ma'am," he said sadly. "I do my best, but the house needs a larger staff. It is hard to keep up appearances."

Rosalys was instantly repentant. She put a hand on his thin arm. "I am sorry. I have the blue-devils, that is all. The room will look much better by candlelight."

Did they have enough candles? No, they did not. When she investigated, she could find only a few partially burned wax tapers. Remembering that Daphne had taken a pair to her room, she went upstairs to get them and found her sister primping in front of the looking glass.

"How do I look, Rosa?" Daphne asked.

She looked very fetching in a mauve challis gown. A violet-colored ribbon decorated the bodice of the dress, and Daphne had used a matching ribbon to catch up her golden curls.

Rosalys kissed her sister's cheek. "You're as pretty as always, Daffy," she said.

"How fortunate that our year's mourning is over, and I may put off my blacks," Daphne said ingenuously. She added, "Mama thinks I must wear my green gown. It is the newest thing I have, to be sure, but I am persuaded that the mauve brings out the color of my eyes. What do you think, Rosa? And, oh, will you lend me your pearl eardrops—the ones that Grandmama gave you?"

Rosalys felt a twinge of regret. "I am afraid not," she sighed.

Daphne looked surprised. "Oh, why? You mean—no, Rosa, *not* Grandmama's ear-bobs too. She gave them to you when you came out. And she died shortly afterward. It is so unfeeling to sell them."

"Pray do not scold me, Daffy." Suddenly feeling weary, Rosalys sat down on the edge of Daphne's bed. She did not like remembering the look in Jason's eyes when he took the collateral, and she fairly writhed at the memory of being assaulted in front of the Royal George.

Then she remembered the picture that that toad had made sitting in the mud, and she couldn't help chuckling.

Her smile brought out a single dimple that emphasized the warm curve of her lips. Daphne looked shocked. "I am not laughing about Grandmama's earrings, Daffy," Rosalys made haste to explain. "I hated to part with them. But really, we needed to have something to serve Dracourt for dinner."

Daphne plopped down on the bed beside her sister. "Food! fuel! I vow I am sick of it all," she cried. "It is horrible to be poor, isn't it, Rosa?"

You don't know the half of it, Rosalys thought. Though Daphne had sacrificed her jewelry and turned her dresses during the past few years, neither she nor their mother understood the difficulty of trying to run a household on next to nothing.

The truth was that they did not want to know. After Sir Henry's loss on the market, the family had attempted to show the world that nothing had changed. Sir Henry had continued to indulge his taste for fine horses while Lady Larrimer had bullied her Bond Street salon to issue credit for new gowns.

Nor had her younger brother worried about pinching pennies. From the first, it had been Rosalys on whom everyone relied. She had been the one who had to dismiss the staff, consult with Cook over meals and pennies, surreptitiously help Angus with his duties, and incur Cook's wrath by frequent personal visits to the butcher, the greengrocer, and the village baker.

"No," she agreed quietly, "it is not pleasant to be poor."

Daphne's rosy fingers pleated the worn satin bed cover as she asked, "Do you think that Dracourt will really offer for me?"

There was an odd note in her voice, and Rosalys looked earnestly into her sister's pretty violet eyes. "Do you loathe the idea, Daffy? I confess I do not care for it above half myself. I will go now and talk to Mama. I will try to persuade her to give up this havey-cavey scheme."

She started to get to her feet, but Daphne stopped her. "I am not sure how I feel," she confessed. "That old letter—it all does seems rather smoky, doesn't it?" Then she added, "But, Rosa, I hate the thought of continuing to be poor. I think it is odious to be without an abigail, and to have to wear clothes that are quite *old*. It is really horrid."

"Then you will not mind marrying the viscount?"

Daphne tapped a finger against a suddenly reddening cheek. "As long as he is not a *complete* horror. And I would *enjoy* being a viscountess. But," she added firmly, "I do not want a husband who goes swimming in his unspeakables. *That* I could not endure"

Rosalys laughed. "You will make a lovely viscountess," she said, and it was true. Had matters been normal, Daphne would have been launched into London society last season and by this time would have been besieged by offers.

Perhaps Mama's scheme was not so foolish after all. Daphne would have her title, and Dracourt would make sure that Larrimer House remained in his wife's family. Because he was so rich, it wouldn't signify that his wife lacked a dowry.

That Dracourt would be pleased with Daphne, Rosalys didn't doubt for a moment. She could not imagine a man alive who wouldn't be enchanted by her sister—unless that man were badly fed. Hungry gentlemen, she knew from experience with her father and brother, tended to behave like bears.

Silently, she offered up a prayer of thanksgiving for the tall groom who had saved the viscount's supper. Now, come what may, they were prepared. Just then, a bloodcurdling shriek erupted from below stairs.

Daphne went pale and clutched Rosalys's arm. "Oh, mercy," she gasped, "what can that be, Rosa?"

As if in answer, Angus tottered up to the open doorway. "I beg your pardon, Miss Rosa, but your presence is required downstairs," he announced. "Cook has burned the meat."

Rosalys sprang to her feet. "Impossible!"

"And there is also a gentleman at the door," Angus continued.

On the point of flying downstairs to face the disaster in the kitchen, Rosalys halted. "A gentleman? What gentleman? What does he want?"

"I have not set eyes on him before today, ma'am. I do not know what he wants." The butler's ancient face was screwed up in disapproval; his Scottish burr reverberated with ill will. "He says his name is Major St. Cyr and that he is expected. He is waiting in the hallway. Miss Rosa, what shall I do with him?"

Chapter Three

"M-Major St. Cyr?"

For a moment, Rosalys's wits deserted her. Her brain felt fogged, and for the life of her, she couldn't think. She stared at Angus, who permitted himself a repressive sniff. "Yes, ma'am. That is the name the gentleman gave."

"But it cannot be. Oh, drat the man—he's a day early!"

"You mean it is—it cannot be D-Dracourt?" Daphne faltered, while Angus turned pale at the realization that he had told a duke's son to wait in the hallway.

Rosalys cut through his stammered excuses. "Never mind, it cannot be helped. Conduct him to the morning room, Angus. It is warm there, anyway. And tell Cook that she must pull herself together."

"She will not do that, Miss Rosa. With the viscount here, and the meat bur-rned—" Angus checked himself, announced hollowly that he would conduct his lordship to the morning room, and exited.

"But, Rosa," Daphne wailed, "my dress is not *ready*."

Rosalys looked down at her own clothes and thought despairingly that she looked like a housekeeper. Her dress of black cotton, unadorned except for its neck ruff of goffered lawn, was hardly an appropriate costume in which to welcome such an important guest.

"It cannot be helped," she sighed.

Daphne was outraged. "Rosa, what *will* he think of us?"

Perhaps Angus had been exaggerating about the meat. If not, there was the mutton stew. Eked out by one of the few surviving bottles of wine, might the mutton be passable?

"No," Rosalys said aloud, "it will not. But it will have to do." She turned to Daphne. "Daffy, you must hurry and tell Mama that the viscount has arrived. She will want to greet him immediately."

"And you?" Daphne quavered.

Rosalys swallowed hard. "I will go down and greet him. We cannot just let him cool his most honorable heels in the morning room."

As she walked down the steps to the first floor, Cook's wail echoed up from the kitchen below stairs. "An' now 'is lordship 'as arrived, and I'm supposed to cook somefink fer 'im," Cook was mourning. "And me with the meat burned, which 'as never happened in thirty year. It's all yer fault, Tom Grady!"

How was Cook's no-account nephew connected with the spoiled meat? Rosalys checked a cowardly impulse to escape into the kitchen and instead crossed the hallway. She walked past the drawing room on one side and the dining room and great hall on the other, and slowly approached the morning room. Here, with her hand on the doorknob, she hesitated.

"Take your fences cleanly," she rallied herself. She gave the door a determined little push.

Angus must have oiled the hinges, for it swung open and disclosed Kedwell's second son.

The Viscount Dracourt was looking out of the west-facing window. He had his back to the door, and she was able to study him unobserved. Afternoon sunlight caught reddish glints in his fair hair, and emphasized the breadth of shoulders clothed in well-fitting gray superfine. His long muscular legs were encased in dark riding breeches and polished Hessians. The hands that were clasped behind his back looked remarkably strong.

Rosalys cleared her suddenly dry throat. "My lord," she began.

He swung around to face her and bowed stiffly, but the light was behind him and partially obscured his features. Her heart sank at his silence. The viscount was probably deep in the sulks over his reception.

Well, if the man didn't introduce himself properly, what could he expect? "Welcome to Larrimer House. I am Rosalys Larrimer. My mother and younger sister will be down to meet you directly." When he still said nothing, she added somewhat desperately, "I am sorry that you did not have more of a welcome, but as you were not expected until tomorrow—"

She broke off, alarmed, as Dracourt smote his forehead. "Tomorrow, was it?" he cried. "Well, hell and damnation, if that don't beat all."

Rosalys started at the familiar voice.

"I beg pardon, ma'am," he continued. "Didn't

mean to swear in front of a lady. I need to be told to sneck up from time to time."

It *couldn't* be. Rosalys stared hard as Dracourt strode across the room toward her. *Oh yes. It could.*

He was saying, "I never have had a head for dates. Thought your lady mother said as I was to come down to Dorset *today.*"

She looked up into familiar, rueful blue eyes set in a sun-browned face and recognized the firm mouth, the set of the strong chin. She could not forget those broad shoulders, the easy, athletic physique. But it was beyond belief that the man she'd thought was a groom had actually been—

"Connor St. Cyr at your service, ma'am," the big man said.

His bow was so deep that it unbalanced him and caused him to bump against the brass table. Some of the gewgaws went tinkling to the floor. Dracourt lunged to retrieve them, and in the process managed to upset the table itself. "Oh, da— I mean, *confound* it," he exclaimed.

"Pray do not concern yourself—I will see to it." Rosalys's heart was still hammering with the shock of recognizing him. It seemed incredible that he hadn't recognized her. But, she thought, as she got down on hands and knees to retrieve the curios, probably it was only natural. No aristocrat, surrounded by servants since he was in leading strings, actually *looked* at such inferiors. Dracourt had naturally never bothered to see past her servant's cloak and bonnet.

Her hands shook as she retrieved the fallen curios. She'd expected Sir Colin Briarwood's grandson to be a little different, but the word was hardly adequate when used to describe Dracourt. He was nothing like his older half brother the present Duke of Kedwell, nor like anyone else she had encountered. Most of the young men who'd courted her during her one London season had been gentlemen of the ton, dedicated to their clothes, their delicate, lead-whitened hands, their prowess at gaming and dancing and racing curricles. There had also been older men, bored and languid and cynical. The viscount was nothing like any of these.

She observed him through her long lashes as she righted the brass table. This afternoon the big man had appeared at ease, a master of the situation. Now he stared uncomfortably at the upset table and shifted from one booted foot to the other.

"No," she cried in real alarm as he began to get down on his knees to help her, "please—I beg you will be seated," Rosalys said. "I will do this. It is much easier if I do so, I assure you."

He gingerly lowered himself into one of the gilt chairs, then pulled out a handkerchief and mopped his forehead. "A great lump, that's me," he confessed. "I may do champion out in the fields, and I can lead a charge like as not. But put me in a lady's parlor and I'm lost, sithee."

This afternoon she had thought he was too fine for his poor clothes. Now she wasn't sure if fine feathers suited him better. Dracourt did not appear comfortable in his well-tailored coat— crafted by no less a personage than Schultz, she was sure—and his snowy cravat was slightly askew.

He gave his forehead another mop and put his handkerchief away. "Your lady mother'll be in a taking," he said frankly. "I don't blame her, mind —I could never abide a guest who came afore his time. Best thing I could do would be to bolt back to that there inn, the Royal George, and come back in the morning."

It was a tempting thought. "Indeed you shall not, sir," Rosalys lied. "We are delighted to have you. My mother will be overjoyed at your arrival."

A quizzical eyebrow rose, and the firm mouth was suddenly humorous. "Do you think so?"

In spite of his rustic manners and speech he was no fool, Rosalys decided. As she rose to her feet she remembered the decisive way in which he'd come to her aid, the way he'd dealt with the drunken fop. No, whatever he was, Dracourt was no fool.

"We are glad to have you," she told him. "Only, we may not be able to entertain you as we would wish."

"Bless you, lass—ma'am, I mean—you needn't worry yourself about that." The tall man leaned back in the chair and crossed his long, booted legs. "No need to entertain me at all. I'm used to tents and soldiers' fare." She raised her eyebrows. "I always insisted on eating what my men ate. Bread and ale'll be champion for me."

Before she could answer, the door of the morning chamber was flung open, and Angus announced: "My Lady Larrimer and Miss Daphne Larrimer."

With Daphne behind her, her ladyship swept into the room, carrying herself with regal dignity. Her graying fair hair had been swept up into a hairdo that resembled a crown, and her black gown of clinging crepe with its ruch of lace and its long train was elegance itself. So was the manner in which she extended her hand in greeting.

"Lord Dracourt," she said, "welcome to Larrimer House."

Her graceful speech was interrupted by a loud crash. Dracourt had shot to his feet, and his abrupt motion had caused his chair to fall backward. He whirled to catch it, failed, and instead banged violently into the settee.

"Oh, mercy," Daphne gasped.

His face red with embarrassment, his lordship drew himself up into a military straightness marred by the lacy antimacassars now draped around his thigh. "Servant, my lady," he exclaimed. "And yours, ma'am," he continued to Daphne.

Lady Larrimer's smile did not falter, but Daphne hastily stifled a giggle. Rosalys saw Dracourt's attention shift to her sister, and watched his embarrassment change to surprise and admiration.

She did not wonder at it. Daphne had changed into an almost-new gown of violet sprigged muslin, and the colors brought out her peaches-and-cream beauty to perfection.

"You have met my older daughter Miss Rosalys

Larrimer," her ladyship was saying. "This is her sister, Miss Daphne Larrimer." As if exhibiting a work of art, she drew Daphne forward, and as the girl sank into a graceful curtsy, added sentimentally, "These girls, sir, are the jewels of my house and the comfort of my old. age."

"Don't you believe it, ma'am," the viscount said kindly. "Where I come from, a woman's judged by her character and not her years. Why, you can be nobbut fifty-five."

Rosalys had never seen her mother at a disadvantage before. "Thank you for such a pretty compliment, my lord," she said acidly.

"Nay, I'm a plainspoken man, any road," he protested. "And never sirrah and 'my lord' me, ma'am. I'm used to being plain Major St. Cyr. Lord Dracourt's a title I haven't grown into, like."

There was a repressive silence. Daphne looked ready to burst into laughter or tears, or both. Lady Larrimer was the picture of affronted aristocracy, and Dracourt looked hopefully at Rosalys, who said rather desperately, "Perhaps we should have some refreshments."

He beamed at her with gratitude. "Now, that's champion. My throat's as parched as the plains of Portugal. It's been hard riding, I can tell you, all the way from Yorkshire."

Lady Larrimer stirred to life. "Ah. Your country seat."

"Don't know as it's any seat. It's my home, sithee." Dracourt paused as Angus tottered in bearing a salver on which were glasses of lemonade and ratafia. Rosalys realized that she was holding her breath as the big man's hand seized one of the glasses, but he did not upset the tray as she had half feared. Instead, as she let out her breath in a sigh, she was aware of the viscount's blue glance on her. He was looking at her for help again.

She thought of the odious fop who had accosted her outside the Royal George and decided that one good turn deserved another. "Mama likes to keep country hours at Larrimer House," she said. "Dinner is usually at five-thirty, sir."

"I hold with that," he replied promptly. "Never got into the habit of setting down to sup at ten or midnight. And I'm a plain man, so don't be worrit about my liking or not liking anything. I've been used to water from a rusty canteen."

Her ladyship winced. Daphne's eyes widened. None of this, thought Rosalys, could be happening.

"It is now half past four." In spite of heroic efforts, her mother's voice was chill. "You will have an hour to prepare yourself for dinner, my lord. Your manservant will have had time to—" She broke off as a horrible possibility occurred to her. "You *do* have a manservant?"

The big man shook his head ruefully. "Nay, I do not, ma'am. Pliskin was nursing an ague, and I hadn't the heart to drag him from his bed." The viscount smiled sunnily and added, "I'll manage champion on my own as long as the old gaffer'll bring up a drap of hot water for me to wash in."

Lady Larrimer opened her mouth to speak but found no words. Rosalys could see her mother's

throat working around a swallow before she
managed to whisper, "We will meet again at dinner, my lord."

She barely inclined her stately head, but he returned the courtesy with zeal. As, with regal dignity, she turned to sweep from the room, he took
a step forward and bowed almost to the floor.

There was the sound of fabric ripping. No one
moved. No one spoke or even dared to breathe.
Into the complete silence Lady Larrimer spoke
through clenched teeth. "Be so good as to remove
your boot from my train!"

Connor St. Cyr looked down. "Oh, bloody
hell," he groaned. "Now I've really gone and
done it."

"Mama, I will not go on with this farce."
Daphne's big eyes were swimming with muti-
nous tears. "The man is a complete block."

Lady Larrimer's lips were pulled into a tight
white line. Her fine hands clasped before her, she
paced the floor of her chamber like a caged ti-
gress. "I cannot credit how strongly Dracourt re-
sembles Sir Colin," she muttered.

"I knew that the man would be queer in the
attic. Not for anything will I entertain the idea of
marrying him."

"Control yourself, Daphne."

Her ladyship's voice brooked no nonsense, and
Daphne subsided. "Block or no, he is the late
duke's son," Lady Larrimer continued. She sank
into a chair near a large and imposing strongbox.
The sight of it seemed to calm her, for after a few

deep breaths, she turned to Rosalys. "Has Cook prepared dinner?"

Rosalys had spent the last half hour in the kitchen, calming the frantic cook and listening to her incoherent excuses. "She has done her best," she said, "but she is anxious about her nephew. Apparently Tom Grady is in some kind of trouble again."

"I don't care a ha'penny for her nephew. I care only that she produce a digestible meal. Not," my lady added bitterly, "that it will matter. Rusty canteen—faugh!"

Daphne covered her face with her hands.

"Go and dress for dinner, miss," her mother ordered. "The man is our guest. Remember that Larrimer House depends on his goodwill."

Silently, Rosalys accompanied her tearful sister to her chamber and helped her dress for the evening. As she murmured soothing rejoinders and offered tactful compliments, her mind ran a worried course between two problems. On one hand there was Cook, stuffing the ruined meat into a pie that she could only hope would be edible. She had never seen Cook so distracted, and she was worried for her.

And if that were not enough, there was a larger problem. "No, he couldn't remember," she murmured. "Not really. He'd have said something if he'd recognized me."

"Rosa, what is the matter with you tonight?" Daphne asked petulantly. "You are jerking my hair." She pushed Rosalys's hands away. "You had better go away and dress yourself for dinner with that clodpole."

"Perhaps his manners will be better after he has eaten," Rosalys said mildly.

Daphne's response was a wail, so Rosalys escaped to her own chamber. Her toilette was simply to braid her hair à la Didion and slip on a dress of unadorned gray taffeta. The time prescribed for mourning might be over, but she wanted to let her sister shine tonight. Recalling the gleam in Connor St. Cyr's eyes when he first saw Daphne, Rosalys hoped that he would please her better at dinner.

But coming down to dinner before the other ladies, Rosalys realized that this was a forlorn hope. One look at the viscount as he waited in the drawing room told her that he was sadly out of place.

Not that the poor man had not done his best. He was dressed in a black swallowtail coat and black knee breeches, his hair had been combed and pomaded smooth, and there was even a gold signet ring on his hand. The problem was that he wore his fine clothes with a careless disregard, and once again his neck cloth was askew. He was fumbling at it when Rosalys came through the drawing room doors. When he saw her, he gave her a rueful smile. "I feel," he told her frankly, "like old man Brankus's pig on market day."

She could not help smiling. "I do not know who Mr. Brankus is, but you bear no resemblance to a pig."

"Nay, lass—I mean, ma'am—you know what I

mean." He pulled at his neck cloth and completely destroyed it. "Pliskins's a dab hand at this, but not me."

There were voices on the stair. Rosalys glanced over her shoulder, then stepped quickly into the room. "If you will stand steady, sir," she said, "I have done this for Jeremy—my brother, you know—many times."

Standing so close to him, she realized how much taller he was than Jeremy. She had to stand on tiptoe to correct the neck cloth. "There, that is much better," she exclaimed.

"It's champion, la—ma'am. I thankee." He had time to say no more, but he sent Rosalys a look of warm thanks as Lady Larrimer and Daphne entered the room.

Her ladyship raked him with a quelling glance before suggesting that it was time that they repaired to dinner. Dracourt did a creditable job of escorting Lady Larrimer into the dining room, but they had hardly sat down at the polished board when Rosalys knew he was in trouble again, for he was looking panicstricken at the array of knives and forks in front of him.

"I'm unused to such grand dinners," he sighed.

"I collect you prefer the rusty canteen." Daphne raised her pert little nose as she administered the snub. "I am surprised that you are not wearing regimentals, sir."

"I sold out some months ago. My mother was sickly at the time, and our lands needed looking after. I had no choice, choose how!" The viscount inserted an uneasy finger between his neck cloth and his strong throat as he added, "It all takes some getting used to, sithee. I feel like a Johnny Raw again."

Lady Larrimer remained ominously silent. Rosalys, taking pity on the big man, picked up the correct fork to show him the way. He shot her a thankful smile, followed suit, and knocked over his drinking goblet.

His clumsiness did not end there. Not only did he upend a water glass into his lap, but he also dropped his knife, and in diving after it lost the fork as well. He also very nearly overturned the heavy soup tureen that Angus was presenting to him

"My father always said as I was hopeless in society," he remarked in apology. "Can't make a silk purse from a sow's ear, they say. Happen that's true."

As if she felt that this had gone far enough, Lady Larrimer cleared her throat. "But you had the best education, my lord. I collect that you were at Eton. Then, if I do not mistake, you were sent up to Cambridge—"

The big man looked horrified. "Steady on, ma'am—you'll make me out a scholar when all I am is a great lump. My head's too thick of learning, any road. If I hadn't been Kedwell's son, I'd have been thrown out on my—I'd have been shown the door."

"But you must have learned *something*," Lady Larrimer exclaimed.

"What I learned came from my grandsire, Sir Colin. He and I got on champion because we thought alike. He taught me to hunt, fish, even swim. Nay, he were a rare one for a swim, Sir Colin."

Daphne choked on her food, and Rosalys said hastily, "Was it your grandfather who suggested that you join the dragoons?"

"Nay, when a man's country is threatened, he needs to fight for it."

He spoke simply but with a sincerity that Rosalys found admirable. "I was glad to buy my colors in the third dragoons," he went on, "and I am glad to have served. But as I told you, my mother needed help with our lands." He paused. "Our land steward is a good man, but I'm one as likes to do for himself. Take my horse, now—I tend to him myself. No groom can do as good as I want done with my Gallant. Why, I rubbed him down myself this afternoon."

Rosalys looked up sharply. The viscount looked as guileless as ever, but she was sure she had not imagined the change in his tone. It was as if he were trying to explain to her why he'd been so poorly clothed this afternoon. If that were the case, it meant that he *had* recognized her.

I need to speak to this man, she thought.

She needed to do it soon—before Dracourt blurted out their "adventure" to Lady Larrimer. Rosalys went cold at the thought.

Lady Larrimer was asking, "You maintain a London residence, do you not, my lord?"

He gave a great shout of laughter. "London? I'd be daft to do that. I never go near that place if I can help it. It's filled with toadies and tulips and

sap-skulls who think they can prove their man-
hood by sparring at Cribb's Parlor."

"You never—go—to London," Daphne repeated faintly. "Then, pray, how do you—what
do you do in the country for amusement?"

"Oh, Yorkshire's a champion place, Miss
Daphne. There's hunting, and fishing, and a fire
o' nights. And there's plenty of fine food, like this
here pie," Connor added as he popped a large
forkful into his mouth. He chewed for some moments and then added thoughtfully, "It's a quiet
life for some, mind you, but a good one for me.
I'd not want any other, any road."

Daphne sagged back against her chair. Lady
Larrimer swallowed several times before saying
firmly, "But when you marry, Lord Dracourt,
your wife will wish to spend the Season at a
fashionable London address. You could not deny
her such harmless pleasures as shopping in Bond
Street, or a box at the opera?"

"I'm not denying anybody anything," he replied firmly, "but you'll not get me to London."

Hurriedly, Lady Larrimer signaled Angus to
bring in a confection composed of day-old bread,
raisins, and country cream. The viscount approved, saying that it was a proper trifle, but nobody else had much appetite. Lady Larrimer
waved the trifle away, and Daphne, whose amethyst eyes signaled thunderstorms, did the same.
Rosalys prayed that the horrible dinner would be
over so that she could get Dracourt alone.

She was grateful when her mother rose to her
feet, indicating the end of the dinner. "We will

leave you to your port and cigars, sir," she said. Then she added hastily, "Pray do not get up."

It was too late. Two water glasses rocked perilously and a plate crashed to the floor as Dracourt sprang to his feet. He bowed, and several knives and forks slid off the table.

Lady Larrimer and Daphne hastily left the room, but instead of following them, Rosalys stayed where she was. "My lord," she began.

"Nay, I've asked you, ma'am—"

"Major St. Cyr, then. If you please, sir, I must speak with you."

"Your servant, Miss Rosalys."

"It is about this afternoon." She added hastily, "You see, it was a mistake. That is to say, I never dreamed—"

She broke off. Her cheeks had grown very warm, and she knew she was blushing. Then she saw that he was looking at her in such a kindly way that some of her confusion died.

"I am making a mess of this," she sighed.

"Nay, words are ungainly things sometimes," he replied. "Like neck cloths."

There was something about the man that put her at her ease. "I needed to go to the butcher's this afternoon," she told him, "so I put on a servant's cloak. You have no idea how the villagers can talk! And—and you recognized me, did you not?"

Before she knew what he was up to, he had reached out to take her hand in his. "Miss Rosalys, it'd take more than a servant's cloak and bonnet to hide your quality. That will always shine through."

Gently, he held her hand. His clasp was strong and warm. "Don't worry about things that don't matter," he told her.

The door of the dining room swung open, and Angus coughed outside. "His lordship's port," he announced gloomily.

Connor St. Cyr gave Rosalys's hand a final squeeze and let it go. "I suppose it won't do me any good to say I can't abide the stuff?" he asked hopefully. "Would you be fatched, old gaffer, if I asked for a bit of ale instead?"

The expression on Angus's face kept Rosalys chuckling long after she had climbed the stairs to her room. Only then did his words come back to her. "It'd take more than a servant's cloak and bonnet to hide your quality," he had said.

It seemed incredible, but the bumbling viscount had just paid her as graceful a compliment as she'd ever received.

Chapter Four

Neither the Dowager Lady Larrimer nor her younger daughter felt equal to coming down to breakfast the next morning, so Rosalys breakfasted alone.

By this time the viscount had long gone. "His lordship is an early riser," Angus announced. "He informed me last night that he is accustomed to breakfasting at seven."

Rosalys looked around her somewhat uneasily. "Where is he now?"

Angus's dour countenance looked longer and even more morose this morning. "His lordship has gone riding. I was given to understand that he will be engaged in this pursuit for several hours."

"That means he will return with a ferocious appetite." Rosalys frowned at her own single slice of toast and sugarless tea.

"The gentleman has a healthy appetite—if I might make so bold, ma'am. Did he make mention—er, did he intimate as to how long his stay might be?"

Rosalys shook her head. Rueful laughter lit her dark eyes as she met the butler's mournful gaze. "I fear that we are in for a long siege, Angus."

Directly after breakfast she went to discuss the matter with Cook. The big woman seemed unusually subdued. "I suppose I can serve the fowl fer nuncheon an' the chops fer dinner," she said, "but what we'll do fer the morrow, Miss Rosa, there's no telling."

"We will have to ford that bridge when we come to it." Cook's nod was so spiritless that Rosalys was alarmed. She put a hand on the big woman's arm. "Is there something wrong? Has Tom really landed in the suds this time?"

Cook's face reddened and she blurted, "That good-for-nowt! He's been a loose stone since he came back from soldiering. You know what they says, Miss Rosa, about rolling stones gathering no moss. But 'e's my dead sister's son, and all I 'ave in the world."

Rosalys waited for her to continue, but Cook had run dry. "And?" she finally prompted.

The big woman glanced uneasily at her mistress. "What Tom wants is money, but 'e's not willing to work fer it like honest folks."

The backdoor banged open as she spoke, and a young man of about twenty-two or twenty-three sauntered into the kitchen. He was a well-made youth, handsome in a flashy way, with a bright scarf knotted around his throat. "Aunty Jane," he began, "I need a favor."

Cook clicked her tongue. "When don't you need a favor, you? And where are yer manners, Tom Grady?"

Made aware of Rosalys, Cook's nephew doffed his cap. "Yer servant, Miss Larrimer," he said. "Didn't know as you was here. I only wanted a word wi' my aunt, if I may make so bold."

Rosalys had never cared for Tom Grady or the way he spoke so humbly while looking her over as if he saw her unclothed. Her voice was cool as she said, "Yes, of course. But you must not upset your aunt."

"Me? I'd never upset Aunty Jane, Miss Larrimer. And I 'eard about your visitor, too," he added glibly. "Be glad to come up to the 'ouse and 'elp out, like. Anyfink for you, miss."

Cook was an open, almost transparent person, and the worry she felt over her nephew was infectious. Rosalys left the kitchen feeling troubled and in that depressed mood began to sweep the hallway.

This was a long-standing practice that called for the utmost delicacy. Angus would have died rather than allow his mistress to touch a broom in his presence, so Rosalys always pretended that while dusting and sweeping she was actually "inspecting" a room. Angus pretended that he believed her.

She had finished the sweeping and was giving the morning room furniture a dusting when Daphne came downstairs. "I declare that I did not sleep a wink all night," she said with a yawn. "I vow that I have such a headache this morning. I must look a fright."

"No, you do not." Daphne actually looked quite fetching in a flocked muslin day gown, and in spite of her complaints, her cheeks were pink with health. "You look as pretty as always," Rosalys soothed.

But Daphne had other things on her mind besides her looks. "Rosa," she said earnestly, "you must help me persuade Mama to give up her havey-cavey scheme. I thought that I might be able to go through with it before I met the viscount. But now!"

Rosalys gave the brass table a wipe with a soft cloth. "He is an original, certainly," she murmured.

Daphne sniffed. "You sound so calm. But then *you* are not being put in a parson's mousetrap so that Larrimer House can stay in the family."

"Keep your voice down, pray." Lady Larrimer entered the morning room, frowned at Daphne, and then turned the same scowl on Rosalys. "Since when have you turned housemaid, miss?"

Rosalys finished her task. "Major St. Cyr's coming has upset our normal routine, Mama," she said quietly.

"Oh, pshaw. And give the man his proper title if you please. His title, after all, is all that is acceptable about him." Lady Larrimer took her accustomed place on her settee, adding, "Angus tells me that Dracourt is riding. When he returns, I intend to discuss the matter of his father's letter."

Daphne threw her sister an imploring look. "Mama, has not this gone far enough?" Rosalys asked. "You admit that there is little to recommend the viscount."

"Daphne will not be the first wife to tutor her husband in acceptable social behavior."

"I do not want to teach him anything!" Daphne wailed.

"Kindly do not make a Cheltenham tragedy out of this," Lady Larrimer warned. "He will be putty in your hands. That type of simpleton always is." She paused to add with deep satisfaction, "Within a few months, he will let you have your own way in all things. The best Bond Street salons will fall over each other to seek your custom. You will have your own box at the opera, your own carriage, a London house with as many servants as you wish. Will you not find that agreeable?"

Daphne clasped and unclasped her hands in an agony of indecision. "He said he would never go to London," she muttered.

"All the better. During the Season, *you* can go to London and he will stay in the country. Would you not like a life of such luxury?"

"You know that I would. I would like that above all things. But I don't want to marry Dracourt to get them. Can I please marry someone else?"

Lady Larrimer almost but not quite sighed. "There is no one else. Resign yourself, Daphne. Marry Dracourt, or we may have to go and live with my Aunt Lakefield."

Before Daphne could react to this ultimatum, there was the sound of hoofbeats. "The viscount has returned," Rosalys said.

"He will come into the morning room to pay his respects." Lady Larrimer drew herself even more erect to meet the challenge. "You girls must stay for a few moments and then go away so that I can speak with him in private."

They fell silent as the door to the morning room swung open, but it was Angus who tottered slowly into the room. In his unsteady hand he carried the silver card tray. "Two gentlemen have come to call, my lady," he announced.

Rosalys glanced at the two cards on the tray. "Lord Edward Padgett," she murmured. "The Honorable Aubrey Windwoode. Do you know either of these people, Mama?"

"I collect that your papa knew a Padgett family. Show the gentlemen in, Angus, and bring up some sherry."

"I regret that there is no sherry left, my lady." Carefully avoiding Lady Larrimer's eye, Angus tottered to the door. "I will bring up some lemonade for the gentlemen."

"You see to what depths we have fallen," Lady Larrimer declaimed mournfully as the butler departed. "In the old days Sir Henry kept the finest cellar in Dorset. Now I am forced to serve lemonade to my guests."

She broke off as Angus announced the callers. Lord Edward, the first to come into the room, was a well-built young man of about twenty-five. He had an open, pleasant face, and his eyes were hazel and merry under dark hair dressed in the fashionable windswept style. He wore his cream-colored buckskins and dark green coat with the same easy grace with which he bent over her ladyship's hand.

"Lady Larrimer," he said, "your most obedient! Had the pleasure of knowing your late husband in London, ma'am. His death is a terrible tragedy. I beg you will accept my most sincere condolences."

"I collect that Henry often spoke your name, my lord," Lady Larrimer said graciously.

"I was out of the country for almost a year," Lord Edward explained. "Only recently heard of your sad loss. Since I was in Dorset, made bold to come and extend. . . . " His words trailed off; his eyes widened. He had caught sight of Daphne.

Though accustomed to adulation, Daphne blushed a little under his lordship's fascinated gaze. She dimpled as Lady Larrimer introduced her daughters. "My lord," she murmured in her soft voice.

His lordship looked stunned for several seconds, blinked hard, and said with some effort, "Beg to present the Honorable Aubrey Windwoode, who came down from London with me."

"Servant, ma'am."

Rosalys stared as Windwoode stepped forward to make his bow. Could she be making a hideous error? But there was no forgetting that voice or that pudgy, self-important figure crammed into a bright blue coat, striped waistcoat, and cravat tied in the waterfall style. No doubt about it—the Honorable Aubrey Windwoode was the same fop who had accosted her outside the Royal George.

As she stared at him, she noticed that a self-satisfied smirk curled Windwoode's mouth. No doubt he considered himself a buck of the first stare and thought that she was fascinated by him. Rosalys didn't know whether to laugh at his impudence or to be relieved that he did not recognize her. There was no question of that here;

Windwoode was the type of man who would never dream that a lady could dress as a maid.

She turned her attention to Lord Edward, who was saying, "Sir Henry was kind enough to invite me to Dorset on many occasions, ma'am. Wish I had accepted long before this. Not every man has the chance to worship at the throne of beauty."

He glanced meaningfully at Daphne, who dimpled and fluttered her eyelashes. Lady Larrimer looked almost beatific. This was the kind of pretty speech that a gentleman should make to ladies.

Angus returned to dispense lemonade. Lord Edward courteously drank the tepid stuff, but Rosalys saw Windwoode sniff his glass and make a wry face. Detestable oaf, she thought.

He was also watching her so intently that she wanted to box his ears. On the pretext of letting in more sunlight, she turned her back to him and went to the window. There she stood for a moment looking out.

The flower gardens were already lush with spring greenery, and from the window she could see the path that led to the riding track that Sir Henry had built for his beloved horses. Once carefully kept by two gardeners and four undergardeners, the track was now choked with weeds and brush. Even so, on a sunny spring morning, it looked irresistible. If only they had been able to afford to keep *one* riding horse, Rosalys thought. If only she could have kept Mirrabelle—

Regret and an aching sense of loss for the old days came sweeping back. Tears pricked her eyelids, and she closed them tightly. When she had mastered herself and opened them, she saw that a solitary horseman had ridden into view. He took a fence then began to canter around the track.

Rosalys was Sir Henry's daughter. Instinctively she recognized the chestnut stallion on the track as a magnificent specimen and its rider as an uncommonly fine horseman. She watched as he approached another fence. This one was a regular stitcher—one that Sir Henry himself had occasionally misjudged—but horse and rider took it cleanly.

"Oh, well done," she murmured.

As if he had heard her, the rider raised his head and looked toward the house, and she saw that it was Lord Dracourt.

For a moment he sat his horse proudly. Then, all at once, the viscount seemed to slump in the saddle. As he rode toward the house, he even appeared to lurch.

"Impossible," Rosalys exclaimed.

"Are you talking to yourself, Miss Larrimer?" The Honorable Aubrey Windwoode had strolled over to stand at the window beside Rosalys. He maneuvered himself so that he actually pressed against her for a moment. Hastily she drew away.

"Our houseguest has returned," she explained shortly.

"My daughter refers to the Viscount Dracourt," Lady Larrimer corrected. "He is staying with us for some days."

"Then I was right," Lord Edward exclaimed. "Drax *is* here." Aware that the ladies were look-

ing at him in astonishment, he explained, "I
heard that Dracourt was in Yorkshire, but when I
visited him there, his mother told me that he was
in Dorset. Devilish fellow for moving about,
Drax. Hoped that I might see him while I was in
the area."

"You know the viscount?" Rosalys exclaimed.

"Drax—Dracourt, I mean—was my officer
when I served in Spain. He was the best officer a
man ever had, give you my word."

Lady Larrimer seemed too astounded for
speech. While she was recovering, heavy boots
punished the floor outside and the door of the
morning room flew open.

"Ned, by God," roared Dracourt.

It was as if a whirlwind had erupted into the
room. The big man strode in, bumped into a
chair, caught the toe of his boot in the carpet, and
brushed against a vase of hyacinths. The vase
crashed to the floor. Water splashed everywhere
and the furniture shook.

Seemingly unaware of the havoc he was caus-
ing, Dracourt reached Lord Edward and wrung
his hand. "I didn't expect to see you in these
parts, Ned," he cried.

"Nor I you, dear old boy. Went looking for you
at Briarwood, but your mother said you had gone
on to Dorset. Fortuitous, since I needed to come
down myself. Bit of business of my late father,
don't you know." Lord Edward's face beamed
with honest pleasure as he added, "Looking top
of the trees, Drax. Cast in the shade by you, give
you my word."

"Nay, it's the country air, lad," Dracourt said with a laugh. Windwoode, who had been watching this commotion with an air of languid disdain, gave a sudden start. "I've been out riding. Gallant gave me a champion race, I can tell thee."

Windwoode lifted a quizzing glass to his eye and examined Dracourt as if he were some species of cockroach. A moment later his glass dropped as from paralyzed fingers. "Good God," he exclaimed.

"Did you say summat?" Dracourt turned and faced Windwoode pleasantly. "Nay, I know you from somewhere. We've met."

Rosalys could have laughed when she saw the expression on Windwoode's face. The fop very obviously recognized yesterday's assailant—and was just as obviously determined to deny this. "N-no," he exclaimed. "Not at all. Assure you. Never clapped eyes on you before in my life."

"Nay?" Smilingly, the big major inspected Windwoode from the top of his pomaded head to the soles of his gleaming Hessians. "I'm like an elephant, sithee," he confided. "I rarely forget a face."

Lord Edward, who had also been staring at the viscount, pulled himself together. "Uncanny memory," he supplied. "Kept us alive on the Peninsula. Once recognized a Frenchy spy even though he was dressed as a Spanish duenna. Spy apprehended—secrets saved—general very grateful." He clapped his big friend's broad shoulder and continued. "My apologies, ladies, for speaking of the war. I've not set eyes on Dracourt since

I sold out last summer. Drax, let me introduce Aubrey Windwoode."

"Ah," Windwoode said. He jerked upright and extended his hand like a marionette. "Quite. Delighted."

"Good to know you, lad." Dracourt grasped the other man's hand in a crushing grip. Windwoode yelped. "Nay," the big man said solicitously, "did I hurt thee?"

Lady Larrimer bit her lip. As Dracourt moved backward and collided with the brass table, she grated, "Pray, sir, be seated."

"No thank you, ma'am. I've been seated on Gallant all morning, begging your pardon, so I'd rather give that part of me a rest."

Lord Edward looked astonished at such coarse speech. Daphne turned away. As Lady Larrimer, pointedly ignoring Dracourt's faux pas, began a conversation with Lord Edward, the viscount strolled over to the Chinese Chippendale daybed, where Rosalys was standing.

"That's a champion riding track but wants attention. You don't ride, ma'am?" She shook her head. "Now, I wonder why. Looking at you, I'd say you could handle the ribbons."

"Indeed?" She spoke coolly, but Dracourt saw the twinkle in her dark eyes. He had once heard that eyes were the windows of the soul, but he had laughed at such flummery until now. Miss Rosalys Larrimer had the most extraordinary eyes he had ever seen. They could laugh, or snap with pride, or fill with the shadows she'd taught herself to conceal behind a smile.

Pluck to the backbone, he thought.

"You enjoy riding, sir?" she was asking.

"Nay, I asked thee—never sirrah me! And I'm not sure as 'enjoy' is the right word. A soldier's horse carries him from place to place. It's a working partnership, you might say."

Lord Edward broke off his conversation with Lady Larrimer to protest this. "Do not let him roast you, ma'am. Drax rides as well as he does other things."

"Indeed," her ladyship murmured.

The viscount smiled easily. "Padgett has a kind nature. He knows as well as you and me that I was put on this earth a slow-top."

"Now, that's doing it too brown," Lord Edward protested. "Why, I remember a time on the Peninsula—" and he launched into a long and colorful description of a military maneuver.

Rosalys leaned against the side of the daybed, watching the two friends. Padgett's talk was making the viscount decidedly uneasy. Dracourt went to stand beside him and tried to interrupt the narrative several times, but his lordship was not a man to be easily distracted.

"Padgett goes on and on, don't he?"

Rosalys realized that Windwoode had come up beside her and again was standing uncomfortably close. She moved a step away. "Does he?" she asked.

Instead of taking the hint, he gave her a self-satisfied smirk. "Interesting oaf, Dracourt. Diamond in the rough, eh? Maybe just the thing for a battlefield, but no place in the drawing room. No ton at all."

He nudged closer again. "Pity that you should be buried out here in the country. 'Pon rep, it would be a pleasure to show you London."

The condescension in his voice made her skin crawl. She tried to walk away from him but could not; she was wedged between Windwoode and the daybed.

"Please," she said coldly, "allow me to pass." He only smiled at her. "I think," she continued even more firmly, "that you presume, sir—"

Before she could finish, a muscular arm swung backward and caught the Honorable Aubrey Windwoode amidships. The stout man grunted, then stumbled backward to collapse on top of the daybed.

Plump booted legs waved helplessly in the air. Daphne uttered a faint shriek, but Rosalys, who thought that Windwoode looked like a beetle on its back, could not hold back her laughter.

Dracourt sprang to his feet. "Oh, damnation, I've done it again," he exclaimed. "Was there ever a blunderbuss like me?"

He strode over to the prostrate Windwoode and hauled him unceremoniously to his feet. "Did I hurt thee, lad?" he demanded anxiously. "Padgett was talking about a cavalry charge, and I got carried away."

Windwoode's reply was unintelligible, but Rosalys saw the venom in his eyes. All thought of laughter died as those eyes met hers. A viper coiled by the road had such a look.

"Hope you weren't afrighted, Miss Larrimer," Dracourt was saying. "I'd think very unkindly of your being discomfited—in any way."

Had she imagined the change in his tone? But she had no time to mull this over as Lord Edward rose to go. "My fault—talked too much and over-stayed our welcome." He bowed over Lady Larrimer's hand. "My lady, your very obedient. Business will keep me in Dorset for some few days—staying at the Royal George along with Windwoode, here—so, with your permission, I would very much like to call again."

Lady Larrimer's assent was cordial. Daphne's smile, as the pleasant young man turned to her, was angelic. "We will be glad to see you, my lord," she murmured.

"Aye, we all will, an' all." Dracourt clapped his friend on the back. "I'll walk thee out, lad."

As the men left the morning room, Daphne sighed, "It looks as if there has been an earth-quake."

It was an accurate description. Water from the downed flower vase was seeping into the carpet and pillows dislodged by Windwoode's collapse had been scattered on the floor. Furniture, disar-ranged by the viscount on his way out the door, added a helter-skelter look.

Lady Larrimer looked sourly about her and commanded Daphne to ring for Angus. "On sec-ond thought, go find him yourself," she ordered then added as her younger daughter left the room, "I may have been too hasty."

Hope soared. "Do you mean that you will give

up this foolishness about Kedwell's promissory note?" Rosalys cried.

"I mean nothing of the kind, but I collect that I must revise my original plan."

Rosalys sighed. "You may as well tell me the whole, Mama."

Lady Larrimer tapped her long fingers on the arm of her settee. "Dracourt was raised by his grandfather in Yorkshire in completely rustic surroundings. Being so far removed from civilizing influences, he cannot be completely blamed for being such a—for being unschooled in the ways of society."

"Do manners make so much difference?" Rosalys mused.

"Of course they do. Manners make the man."

"And clothes, and money. Since a man like Mr. Windwoode has both, he's accounted a gentleman. Our society seems to be wanting in the top story."

"Fustian! You are rainbow-chasing today, miss." Lady Larrimer knit her aristocratic brows. "The important thing is that manners can be learned. I am persuaded that Lord Edward can work wonders with his friend if he but has the chance. Perhaps he can even convince him to employ a manservant who can tie a cravat properly."

"All this is leading to something," Rosalys said. Lady Larrimer told her. "A dinner party? Mama, you are funning me. Do you know how much food we would require?"

"It would be a small party," Lady Larrimer said stubbornly. "We are only out of our blacks and can scarce be expected to entertain on a grand scale. I will invite our neighbors, Colonel Montfort and his wife. He was your dear papa's friend, and Mrs. Montfort is a kind woman. Besides, the colonel, being a military man, may be able to entertain Dracourt and keep him—well, out of harm's way."

"Very well," Rosalys said resignedly. "Who else besides the Montforts? I collect you said a 'party.'"

"Naturally, we would ask Lord Edward. And it would be rude not to include his friend."

Rosalys opened her mouth to protest this but did not do so. There was no possible way she could tell her mother about that scene outside the Royal George.

"As to expense, I am not such a fool as to be unaware of our straits. But I still have a diamond stickpin that belonged to your papa. Angus will have to take it to town. Go up to my room, Rosa, and bring me my jewel case, if you please."

Obediently, Rosalys went upstairs. As she walked toward her mother's room, she was surprised to meet the viscount in the upstairs hallway. He was striding toward Lady Larrimer's chamber.

Was he lost? His walk was brisk and sure, however, and she glimpsed a purposeful expression on his finely chiseled profile.

"Sir?" Rosalys queried.

He turned quickly, saw her, and was transformed. Stumbling, he lost his footing and had to save himself by clutching at her mother's half-open door.

"Yes, Miss Larrimer?" he asked. "Can I do summat for you?"

He sounded helpful and eager to please. Looking at him searchingly, she met eyes that were clear and as innocent as a baby's. "You were going into my mother's room," she pointed out.

He looked around him vaguely, then smacked his thigh with his big hand. "By God it's true. Now, how can that be? Eh, I was going toward my room and lost my way, like. I'm that absent-minded."

"Are you?" she murmured.

He smiled. "Why, I'm a cabbage-head. Happen I'd get myself lost in my own house."

It was on the tip of her tongue to tell him that she did not believe him, but before she could do so, she heard Angus's slow steps coming up the stairs. It was a situation she did not want to air in front of the old butler. "I hope you can find your own quarters now," she said.

He smiled sheepishly and wandered off. She watched his stumbling progress for a few seconds and then warned herself not to get into a taking. Viscount Dracourt might very well be the guileless slow-top he appeared to be.

But somehow she didn't think so.

Chapter Five

Viscount Dracourt came down the stairs even earlier than was usual. The servants were still abed, and except for the creaking sounds normal to an old house, there was silence. As he passed the landing, he glanced up at the painted visage of the late Sir Henry.

The old baronet looked dyspeptic and glum, and well he might considering the goings-on in his home. Dracourt himself had been shocked to learn just how pinched in the pocket the Larrimers were.

The landlord of the Royal George had been a mine of information, telling him that the parkland that had bordered the estate east and west had been cut into parcels of farmland and sold. The woods that formed the northern periphery were apparently still held by the family, but both they and the riding track that skirted them had been sadly neglected. And daffodils and primroses couldn't disguise the fact that gardeners were no longer employed at Larrimer House.

But none of this had been as bad as the stables. Dracourt frowned now, remembering the weeds that had taken over the cobbled yard, the paint that had blistered and flaked on the doors, the mildew that caked the inner walls. Sir Henry's blood horses and hunters had once been the talk of Newmarket. Now the stalls were empty except for one ancient cart horse.

" 'Imperial Caesar, dead and gone to clay,' "

Dracourt mused as he looked about the sleeping
house. Built of strong Ham Hill stone, Larrimer
House had held up much better than its ravaged
surroundings. The stone had weathered to a
warm gold and the oak beams and floors glowed
like dark silk. This old house, he thought, could
sparkle if it got the care it deserved. But with
only two ancient servants, the place was choking
to death.

It was a coil and no mistake. On the one hand,
there was his father's note. On the other—

An odd, scraping sound came from the dining
hall. Dracourt stopped in mid-thought and for a
second stood listening. Then, moving as lightly as
a cat, he crossed the hallway, passed the brooding
great hall, and pushed open the dining room
door.

He saw Rosalys staring up at the stained-glass
windows. She had just finished maneuvering a
wooden ladder into place and was catching her
breath. A bucket of soap and water at her feet
announced her intention to clean the windows—
a truly formidable task. They were ceiling-high
and latticed with hundreds of grime-encrusted
green and amber panes.

Rosalys gave the ladder a determined shake. It
creaked alarmingly and she pushed it into better
position, testing it again. Then, before Dracourt
could stop her, she'd bunched up her skirts,
picked up the bucket, and begun to climb the ladder.

It was a difficult business. She had to hold to
the ladder with one hand while balancing her

bucket with the other. Afraid to startle her, Dracourt held his peace as she made her way to the top of the ladder, hung her bucket on a sturdy nail that had been hammered into the ladder's side, and reached inside the bucket for a sponge.

This slight movement was her undoing. Rosalys felt the ladder shift under her. Instinctively she clutched the slopping bucket and braced herself for a fall.

But she did not fall. Instead of crashing to the floor, the ladder miraculously steadied. "Are you all right, Miss Larrimer?" Dracourt's deep voice demanded below her.

How had he got here? But there he was, steadying the still-swaying ladder. "Thank you," Rosalys managed. Her heart had begun to beat violently, and she had trouble forming words. "I —I think I turned too quickly and unbalanced the ladder."

"It wouldn't take much to do that. You're daft to be climbing up this thing," he told her bluntly.

All she could think of was, "It is the only ladder we have."

A spark of humor filled his worried blue eyes, and the firm mouth softened. "Best come down. You'll be falling, else, and will break some bones."

"But I would not make the same mistake again."

"Are you coming, or do I have to climb up and carry you down?"

The idea of the big man clambering up the already teetering ladder was so absurd that she smiled. "We would both fall, then," she told him.

"Nay, but you'd fall atop of me, and that's a lot of padding." Dracourt held out a big hand. "Come down, wilta? Not," he added, with a grin, "that you don't look a fetching sight up that ladder, but it isn't safe."

She was suddenly aware of how her skirts were bunched up revealing her ankles. Hastily, she climbed down and rearranged her clothing. "Why are you up so early?" she demanded. "I was persuaded that everyone was asleep."

He nodded wisely. "Ah. You thought you were safe from Angus."

"Well—" She hesitated then added frankly, "The last time he tried to clean these windows, he fell and had back spasms for a week. But Mama said that the panes were filthy and would not do for tonight's gathering. So Angus was going to attack them today."

"What about that gormless lad—Cook's nephew?" Dracourt wanted to know.

"Tom Grady? I wish I knew," she sighed. "Cook asked him, and he said he'd come yesterday, but we've not seen hide nor hair of him."

"Mark you, I'd not trust that young fellow farther nor I could throw him. There's something of a Captain Sharp about that boy." Dracourt glanced critically up at the tall windows. "So your lady mother's in a taking over tonight."

It was hardly an exaggeration. Lady Larrimer was preparing for tonight's party as earnestly as if it were the most important event of the season.

Cook threatened to have convulsions if her lady-ship changed the menu one more time, while the state of the Brussels lace tablecloth had nearly thrown Lady Larrimer into a decline. Now, thankfully, things were calmer. The menu was set, and the Larrimer ladies had sat up late to mend the tears in the tablecloth.

Rosalys looked uncertainly at her tall companion. "Tonight is important to Mama," she tried to explain. "This is the first time we are entertaining guests since Papa died. She wants everything perfect because—" She hesitated.

"Because everything else is not perfect?" he suggested.

"Yes, that is exactly what I mean. Mama can pretend that she is hoaxing you into believing that we are living in the lap of luxury, but you cannot be blind. Besides, I saw you carrying the coal scuttle for Angus yesterday. You *know* the way things stand."

He looked embarrassed for a moment, then shrugged. "Well, talking never mended fences. We'st best get to work."

Before she could think what he was up to, he had thrown off his jacket, rolled up his shirt-sleeves, and assaulted the ladder. She stretched out a hand with the vague notion of stopping him, but by then he was already sponging the topmost pane. "Hold the ladder steady," he commanded. "Throw your weight into it—that's it."

Too astonished to argue, she obeyed and watched him work. He sponged, washed, and wiped with incredible efficiency. She could not help protesting feebly, "But—but you must not do this!"

"Why not? I've washed many a window at Briarwood," he confessed.

"Don't you have *servants* in Yorkshire?"

"My grandfather believes that one should know how to do a job before giving it to a servant." He paused to look critically at his work. "That will do for these panes. We'll have to move the ladder, lass."

She protested this. "That we will not. I did not mean for you to wash windows."

"Why not?"

"Why *not?* It is not proper, for one thing, and for another, you are our guest."

He grinned down at her. "Precious proper guest I am, an' all. Now, lass, don't you have anything else to do but fiddle with windows? There'll be flowers to arrange, I'll be bound. Females are forever arranging flowers."

"But we must do so since you are always knocking them down," she retorted. He threw up a hand, acknowledging the thrust. "Yes, there are flowers to arrange in the drawing room, if you must know. And do not call me 'lass.'"

"Nay, it slipped out!" Dracourt descended from the ladder and added, "The drawing room windows'll need washing, too."

"If Angus ever saw you doing his work—"

"Hold fast, lass—I mean, ma'am. Angus won't know." One big hand covered hers reassuringly. "We must be done before t'old bubble turns his head on his pillow."

"But he will see the windows!"

"You can look at him innocent-like the way you do when you're doing the dusting or sweeping for him," Dracourt pointed out.

The man knew too much. What else was going on behind that guileless expression? Rosalys saw the odd look on his sun-dark face and the light in his eyes, and had a horrible thought. Was Lord Dracourt presuming to *pity* her?

The pride of the Larrimers, stiff necked and centuries old, smarted under the lash of that thought. Realizing that his hand still covered hers, she quickly pulled it away. "We can take care of our own, my lord," she told him coldly.

When her eyes flashed like that, Dracourt thought, and with that rose damask color staining her fine, high cheekbones, she was lovely. She was not merely beautiful like the candy-box miss upstairs, nor as alluring as the many women he had met and admired and sometimes loved a little. Rosalys Larrimer's loveliness went much deeper; it would be with her, never dimming, until she died.

She was pluck to the backbone and just now as resty as a mare of finest blood. "I know you can deal with what you have on your plate," he told her. As she drew her slender figure even straighter, he added gently, "But it goes against my grain, think on, to watch a woman work while I stay idle. Besides, I have not had my exercise this morning."

"Then you should ride," she told him tartly.

"There's time for all that. Come off your high

ropes, lass, and let me clean the windowpanes, wilta?"

Her spasm of pride was swiftly fading in the face of his smile. "You are impossible, sir. And— and what your mother would think of this I do not know."

"Like as not she'd hitch up her skirts and be up the ladder herself. Eh, she's a gradely lass, my mother."

His tone was so warm that she forgot her annoyance. As he easily hefted the ladder and walked toward the drawing room, she wondered what his childhood had been like. How had "that most peculiar young woman," as Lady Larrimer put it, reared him?

"You spent your childhood in Yorkshire, did you not, my lord?" she asked.

"Aye, I did. Bring the bucket of suds, wilta? And," he continued, "there's another thing. Did I not tell you to stop sirrahing and my-lording me in that toplofty way? My name is Connor."

"Surely you know it would be improper to address you in that way."

"Maybe not when I'm dressed up like a plum pudding and sitting in the drawing room, but while we are washing windows, why not?"

She had to laugh. "You are the most complete hand," she admitted. Then she added, "Well, here is the drawing room—and the windows."

He groaned. "By Gow, I'd like to get my hands on the man who built this place! Couldn't he have made one wall without putting a window in it?" He set up the ladder and began to climb again. "Hold it steady, now."

"Indeed I will. If you fall, there will be water all over the floor."

He grinned down at her. "That's my lass."

"I am no such thing." But she smiled as she said it. There was nothing underhanded about this man, no hint of the slyness that marred Windwoode's gestures and looks. "You have a strange way of speaking, my lord."

He paused in mid-wipe. "You're doing it again. You're no want-wit, so you should have learned my name by now. I tell you what," he added, "next time you call me 'my lord' or 'sir,' I'll exact a penalty from you."

"Indeed!"

"Aye, *indeed.* If you doubt me, try." The gleam in his blue eyes told her that he looked forward to the penalty, whatever it was. Then his blue gaze rested on her lips, and understanding made her flush indignantly. But before she could tell him what she thought of him, he was adding, "As to my way of speaking, there's nowt wrong with plain talk. I'm tired of mushrooms and toad-eaters and simpering debs. Give me a man or a woman who'll say 'aye' or 'nay.' I'll take that any day afore I'll take the gibberings of a counter-coxcomb like that Windwoode."

She frowned a little. "I have not yet thanked you for your intervention."

"Nay, there's nowt to thank me for. I did nowt. A proper gowk I must have looked, knocking that young tulip head over heels."

She chuckled. "He looked like a turtle on its back."

"He won't plague you again. You can rely on it."

The tone of his voice had not altered, but she sensed the steel beneath the easy, good-humored veneer. Suddenly serious, she said, "I wanted to box that odious Mr. Windwoode's ears, believe me. And you did it all so cleverly—it seemed an accident. But—but he knew it was not by chance. He was furious. If you had seen his eyes!"

He did not comment but began to wash vigorously. Rosalys reflected that no one seeing this swift, sure man would believe he was the bumbling Viscount Dracourt. Only, of course, there had never been a bumbling viscount. She wasn't sure about his quaint way of speech—perhaps that was an authentic Yorkshire accent—but everything else about Connor St. Cyr had to be a hoax.

"You're silent, lass," Dracourt said.

"I was admiring your work."

Why he was trying to bamboozle them was obvious. Any man of spirit—and she knew Dracourt had spirit enough to spare—would have been in a taking over his father's promissory note. Dracourt was hoping that Lady Larrimer would tire of his bumpkin antics and give up her scheme.

It was on the tip of her tongue to tell him that she had seen through his ruse, but something held her back. She was not completely certain, for one thing. And there was another, more elu-

sive reason. Rosalys did not want to spoil the ease
and warmth that had grown between them.

He was saying, "I'm glad to hear I'm passing
muster. Sir Colin always said as the laborer was
worth his hire."

She was intrigued. "Really? I heard that Sir
Colin had rather—unusual views about things."

Dracourt descended from the ladder. "Don't
you mean that some think him as mad as Dick's
hatband?"

"Of course not. But he is said to have swum in
his—" She checked herself in time.

"Ah, grandsire's morning swim. Proper famous
he was for that, mind you, and the talk of the
county. But I'll tell you that if a dip in the water
could give 'un the iron constitution that old man
had, I'd jump in with my boots on." He reposi-
tioned the ladder then added, "Sir Colin might
have had his ways, but he were a man who
would harm no living thing willingly. 'Each thing
that lives has the right to be happy,' he taught me
when I was a little shaver."

Listening to Dracourt's deep voice, she could
picture the scene. Sir Colin, gray haired but pink
cheeked and hale; the sturdy, small boy with the
bright, eager eyes who would one day grow into
this tall man. "He sounds like a kind person," she
murmured.

"He was. But he had a temper, too." Dracourt
swished his sponge reminiscently. "I'll tell you
about one thing that happened when I was a little
lad. One of our gardeners had a daughter, a
pretty young lass and a good girl. But a neighbor

of ours—I won't be telling names, but he was a grand lord with a famous title—decided to have a bit of fun in the petticoat line. He went so far as to abduct that young lass."

"Infamous! What did Sir Colin do?"

"He paid a call on the fellow and confronted him. When the fool would not turn the lass loose, my grandfather horsewhipped him."

"Oh, well *done,* Sir Colin," Rosalys cried. "But did this neighbor not have the law after your grandfather?"

"A man does not like to admit he has been horsewhipped by a man weighing several stone less than he. No, we had no trouble from him afterwards—and neither did the girl."

Rosalys murmured, "Ah," and wondered if he realized that in remembering the old story, Dracourt had forgotten his broad Yorkshire accent.

He remembered immediately afterward, however, for he said, "That's gone and done it, then. No more windows! But I'll need to come back and give t'gaffer a hand later on in the day. The furniture is too heavy for him to move alone."

"You cannot do that," she cried in alarm. "Angus would be boiled in oil rather than let you help him."

"Nay, lass, do you think I'm completely gormless?" Descending the ladder, he put a friendly hand on her shoulder. "T'gaffer's interested in battles. All I need to do is to map out a campaign on the Peninsula. The sofa will be the Frenchys, and the chairs our men. By the time we all retreat and advance, the furniture'll be rearranged and none'll be the wiser."

She knew she should protest the hand on her shoulder, but she did not. It conveyed a sense that she was no longer alone in an unequal battle. Moved by the camaraderie of the moment, she clicked her heels together in what she thought might be a military manner.

"As I have said before, you are a *complete* hand," she said, and watched the sunlight dance through the newly cleaned windows into his smiling blue eyes.

The morning sun gave way to clouds, and by evening there was a sea wind that brought rain and fog. But there was unaccustomed warmth and cheer inside Larrimer House since her lady-ship had decreed that, economy be damned, a hearty fire should welcome the guests in *both* the drawing room and the dining room.

The fire in the dining room roared with a will and drowned out the dreary sound of rain. In the afternoon Angus had polished all the brass, and Daphne and Rosalys had filled every available vase with spring flowers. Even the chairs had been vigorously brushed and looked uncom-monly fine.

The guests might not have noticed these small touches, but when they sat down to dinner, Rosalys's anxious eyes could find nothing amiss. The table was set magnificently with ancestral china and Cook, by dint of working like a vol-cano in the kitchen, had created a feast. Lady Lar-

rimer wore a look of rare content, and when Mrs.
Montfort praised the pickled crab, her ladyship
beamed.

The Montforts were not the only ones to appreciate Cook's genius. The Honorable Aubrey
Windwoode had devoured large helpings of mutton and beef and was now demolishing one of the
last bottles of Sir Henry's Madeira. Lord Edward,
however, had hardly touched his plate. Seated
across from Daphne, he was too busy telling her
about a play he had seen at the Lyceum Theater.
Under his attentive gaze she looked happier than
she had in months.

And so far Dracourt had not misused his silver,
upset his water glass, or caught the sleeve of his
fine blue coat in the gravy. Rosalys suspected that
this was because of their earlier conversation, and
was grateful that he was not spoiling things for
her mother.

By the time the gentlemen, finished with cigars
and port, had joined the ladies in the drawing
room, a mellow mood had fallen on everyone.
Only Lady Larrimer remained energetic enough
to suggest a rubber of whist. "Lord Dracourt, you
and Daphne must be partners," she commanded.

Dracourt looked alarmed. "Nay, I'm a poor
hand at cards. Ned's got a much better head than
I."

Lord Edward pronounced himself honored to
be Daphne's partner. "Not such a great player,
give you my word, but Miss Larrimer would inspire a block of stone," he announced.

Daphne blushed as his lordship's hazel eyes

smiled into hers. "I am not so good a player either, my lord," she said timidly.

The Dowager Lady Larrimer was having none of this. "Nonsense. My daughters are very good at whist. Daphne will teach you the ropes, Lord Dracourt. You will partner Rosalys, Lord Edward, if you please."

But Lord Edward had been a military man. He showed remarkable courage in defying her ladyship's decree and instead drew his chair between Dracourt and Daphne, saying he would coach his friend. This left Mr. Windwoode to be Rosalys's partner.

"Now, Miss Larrimer, I have you where I want you," he drawled.

She knew what he meant a moment later as, under the table, she felt his knee seeking hers. Was she mistaken? No, the man's pudgy knee was definitely nudging hers suggestively.

"Pray, Mr. Windwoode, your chair cannot be comfortable," she said with mock solicitude. "You are shifting and moving so. Perhaps this straight-backed chair may be more to your liking."

Windwoode merely smirked. " 'Pon rep, ma'am, I am well suited."

"Are you, by Gow?" Dracourt asked. "Nay, lad, tha'rt brave to sound so confident."

Windwoode opened his mouth to reply and met steely blue eyes. He coughed, then forced a laugh. "I only meant that Miss Larrimer and I will do our best to beat you," he mumbled.

He gave her no more trouble after that, but Rosalys knew the fop was seething.

It did not help that the game was uninspired. As he had warned, Dracourt was a terrible player and lost trick after easy trick. "I warned you, Miss Daphne," he sighed. "I'm a proper noodle-head, so I am."

Windwoode sneered. His playing was much better than anyone else's, and either because of this or because of her earlier snub, he had no patience with his partner. Once she threw a wrong card, and he snapped, " 'Pon rep, ma'am, can't you keep your mind on the cards?"

Rosalys flushed at his tone but answered peaceably, "I am persuaded that you are right. I am a sad partner, I fear."

But Lord Edward would not have this. "Nothing of the kind—you play very well, Miss Larrimer." He gave her a warm smile then added repressively, "Your fault, Windwoode, for trying that finesse. Devilish things, finesses. Never turn out the way you want them to."

He turned to compliment Daphne on a clever play. Daphne had been having a trying evening, but now her amethyst eyes went soft with pleasure. "You are too kind, my lord," she told him. "You are joking me, I think."

Lord Edward's ruddy cheeks went even redder. "Assure you—not joking at all," he said fervently. "You are a fine player, ma'am."

"Nay, especially when I was your partner," Dracourt interjected. "If anyone was handicapped by such a wooden-head! I'd as lief ride to hounds on a mule as play whist wi' me."

Colonel Montfort, who had gone to sleep in a corner of the room, jerked awake at this. "Hounds—ha!" he exclaimed. "Hunt, do you?" Dracourt allowed that he did—a little. "Used to hunt in the shires, had a lodge in Leicestershire," the colonel continued. "I hunted with the Quorn in my time."

"That was a long time ago," his lady said deprecatingly. "Even so, we maintain an adequate stable—though not as good as Sir Henry's is—I mean, *was.*"

Mrs. Montfort looked embarrassed, so Rosalys made haste to cover her small slip. "Papa always admired your hunters, ma'am. And he said you kept the best hounds in the county."

"No more than we envied him his blood horses!" Mrs. Montfort smiled gratefully at Rosalys. "Now that your year is up, my dear, you must ride again. I collect you rode very well indeed."

Lady Larrimer whisked out a black-edged handkerchief and looked hard at her daughters. "Perhaps one day all of us will ride again."

Perhaps one day, when we have hunters in the stable again! Rosalys read the message plainly, but the colonel, alarmed at the thought of possible tears from the widow, attempted a diversion. Turning to Dracourt, the colonel said, "Third Dragoons, eh? Top of the trees horsemen in that regiment. I insist you ride to hounds with us at our next meet. Wednesday, that would be."

Mrs. Montfort suggested that the ladies join the hunt. Lady Larrimer declined, saying that they had just shed their blacks. "Then you must come and *watch* the meet and join us for luncheon afterward," Mrs. Montfort insisted. She smiled at Dracourt, adding, "I promise you that you will approve of our country sport, Lord Dracourt. And will you come also, Mr. Windwoode?"

Windwoode looked bored. "I am used to hunting in the shires," he drawled. "However, in the country, I suppose, one must seek provincial pleasures."

"And you, Lord Edward?"

Lord Edward was deep in conversation with Daphne, so the question had to be repeated twice. When he exclaimed "Eh?" the invitation was extended a third time, and he accepted with endearing pleasure. "Good of you—I would like it above all things. Nothing as invigorating as a hunt, by Jove. Hounds catching the scent—"

"The notes of the horn," Mrs. Montfort added, smiling.

"The viewhalloo," the colonel cried. Getting into the spirit of the moment, he added dramatically, "And then there is the pound of horses' hooves, eh? Nothing like it in the world."

As if in echo of his words, hooves beat outside in the courtyard. Immediately thereafter, the front door crashed open. All the gentlemen sprang to their feet, and Daphne shrieked and caught hold of her sister's hand.

Now they could hear Angus's voice expostulating in the hall. "No, sir, really, you canna go in thur-re looking like that—"

"What on earth?" Rosalys exclaimed.

The drawing room door banged open and a fierce figure, booted, spurred, and wearing a thick dark cloak, stood on the threshold. For a moment he remained motionless, then, like an avenging spirit, he strode into the room.

"I say, hold on a moment," Lord Edward challenged.

Without paying the slightest attention, the cloaked figure leveled a finger at Lady Larrimer.

"I have heard about your sheep-brained scheme," he accused. "It will not do. Hang it, Mama, I will not let you go through with it!"

Chapter Six

Lord Edward blinked. "Mama? Then this young man is—"

"Our odious younger brother, sir," Rosalys sighed. "Jeremy, what do you mean by this idiotic performance?" An awful possibility occurred to her. "You have not been sent down from Oxford for some prank?"

The boy colored. "Pray do not be a gudgeon, Rosa. I ain't been rusticated. I am here because I heard about Mama's cockle-brained scheme. I tell you, I am not about to—"

"Jeremy!"

Jeremy Larrimer stopped in mid-sentence.

"I did not expect you home, my son," Lady Larrimer continued in the same compelling tones. "You must be weary after your long journey. Did you come by chaise?"

Jeremy shook his dark head. He was a lanky youth, all but grown but not yet filled out. He had, Dracourt observed with interest, Rosalys's coloring, high cheekbones, and dark eyes. They sparked indignantly as he replied, "No, I rode."

"All the way from Oxford!" Daphne exclaimed.

"How foolhardy," Lady Larrimer sniffed. "No wonder you are splashed with mud. Rosalys, ring for Angus, if you please."

"But, *Mama!*"

"You were about to say you had not been introduced to our guests." Dracourt had to admire the way her ladyship took the stripling in hand. Jeremy was a wild colt and just now quivering with affront, but he did not dare argue with his mother. "This gentleman is Lord Edward," Lady Larrimer said.

"Padgett," Lord Edward said kindly. "Glad to make your acquaintance, Larrimer. Happy to be of service."

Gratefully, Jeremy shook his lordship's outstretched hand and looked somewhat sheepish as he acknowledged Windwoode and made his bow to Mrs. Montfort and the colonel. "Did not see you," he stammered. "The fact is I was in such a hurry that I didn't notice anyone was in the room."

"Hard riding will do that to you sometimes," Lord Edward said cheerfully, and Mr. Windwoode, who had been examining Jeremy through his quizzing glass, agreed.

"Next time you undertake a long journey, drive, do not ride," he drawled. "'Pon rep, my grays make nothing of distance."

"Oh, are those high-steppers outside *yours?*" Jeremy began eagerly when his mother intervened.

"You have not yet been made known to the viscount. Lord Dracourt, my son."

The boy's eyes narrowed. His nostrils flared. Instead of shaking the big man's hand, he put his behind his back.

"Sir," he snarled.

Rosalys bit her lip and glanced at Dracourt. Jeremy's rudeness appeared to have flustered him so badly that he stammered, stepped backward, bumped into a table, and sent a candle stand toppling into Daphne's lap.

Lord Edward made a heroic leap and caught the candles before they fell. "Do be careful, dear old boy," he said, gasping. "Miss Larrimer—beg pardon if I startled you—you've taken no hurt?"

Daphne's answer was lost in Dracourt's penitent groan. "There, see that? It's a good thing that Ned was by. You may have burned up, ma'am. Big lummox that I am, I can't even move without turning things topsy-turvy."

Jeremy looked startled. Windwoode snickered and raised his quizzing glass. Lord Edward looked hard at his friend, then turned away.

"But it's your fault, young'un," Dracourt accused. "You came through that door looking like a proper highwayman or like one of your local smugglers."

Jeremy stared haughtily at the tall viscount. "There are no highwaymen in *these* parts—nor smugglers, either. You're talking moonshine—*sir.*"

"But he's not." Lord Edward rallied to his friend's defense. "There's a riding officer just come from London at the Royal George."

"A mushroom," Mr. Windwoode sneered.

"But why would he be here?" asked Rosalys, astonished. "The 'Brethren of the Coast' have not been active here for years."

"That is not what that riding officer said. Now, what *were* his name, Ned?" Lord Edward shook his head. "Dosta remember, Windwoode?"

" 'Pon rep, I do not pay attention to the name of every jackanapes I brush up against," Windwoode said witheringly. "You are the one with the good memory. Or so you say."

"Merchum, that were it. You should do summat about your memory, lad. Happen it will keep you out of trouble some day."

Windwoode's retort was checked by the arrival of Angus. "May I take your cloak and hat, Master Jeremy?" the old butler burred disapprovingly. "If you will come with me, preparations have been made in your chamber. For your *ablutions,* sir."

Jeremy gave in with as good grace as possible. He made his bow to everyone, pointedly ignored Dracourt, and left the room. Rosalys saw the tall viscount looking thoughtful and asked, "Are you serious about smugglers being active here in Dorset?"

"Aye, I am."

"I had heard stories that there was smuggling here years ago. The tidesmen sometimes could not land their goods on the coast, so to escape detection they would bring their cargo up the Stour."

"Not surprising the beggars are active again," Colonel Montfort put in. "The war, you know. Goods brought in without the tax means profit."

Daphne looked alarmed. "Do you think that it might become dangerous?"

Lord Edward made haste to reassure her. "You are perfectly safe, Miss Larrimer. Besides—comes to that—you have only to command me in anything."

Daphne's cheeks pinkened and her long lashes fluttered. "You are so kind, Lord Edward. But the thought of those odious men makes me feel quite faint."

Lady Larrimer had had enough of smugglers. "Lord Edward is perfectly right," she said crisply. "There is no danger at all, so pray do not be a pea-goose, Daphne." She turned to her guest, adding, "Mrs. Montfort, if you mean your kind invitation, I am persuaded that the girls will enjoy viewing the hunt. Can that be arranged?"

Talk turned at once to the proposed hunt. The plans took a long time, and Rosalys was aware of her mother's growing impatience. Her ladyship wore a fixed smile and kept glancing at the clock on the little side table. When the guests finally took their leave, she told her daughters that she wished them to meet in her chamber. "Jeremy owes us an explanation," she declared.

Rosalys agreed that her brother had been very disobliging, but when he faced his mother and sisters in Lady Larrimer's room some time later, she could not help feeling a little sorry for him. Washed and combed and divested of his cloak and riding boots, Jeremy looked much younger even than his seventeen years.

Yet his determination was unshaken. "Mama," he plunged in immediately, "this is a rum business. What made you take up this hubble-bubble scheme to marry Daffy to that big nodcock?"

"Have you finished?" her ladyship asked ominously.

"No, I ain't! Hang it, this is the most yawl-rigged caper," Jeremy cried indignantly. "Dracourt's an oaf."

"Oh, thank you, Jeremy!" Daphne threw her arms around her champion, who spoiled the effect by advising her to take a damper.

"Why haven't you put a stop to this, Rosa?" he demanded. "You haven't gone on the toodle, have you?"

Lady Larrimer's eyes narrowed to dangerous

slits. Rosalys hastily asked, "How did you hear that Dracourt was here?"

"Chap I go to school with is related to Dracourt's family. His manservant got the word from Dracourt's mother's maid about Kedwell's promissory note. You know how servants talk," Jeremy concluded wrathfully. "How do you think I feel looking like a cake among my friends?"

"You have said quite enough, I think," her ladyship said.

Jeremy was a tall boy, topping Daphne by a full head and Rosalys by several inches, but under his mother's glare, he seemed to shrink.

"I'm a downy one, Mama," he muttered. "I know it is a rum go at home and that we are short of blunt since Papa died. But to try and cozen someone like Dracourt into dangling after Daffy because of a letter—that is going it too brown. If he were a regular fellow it might be something, but to saddle Daffy with a want-wit who can't keep from tripping over his own feet is the outside of enough."

There was a short silence. Rosalys was surprised when seconds passed and her ladyship continued to hold her peace. Instead of withering her offspring with a few well-chosen words, Lady Larrimer turned her back and walked deliberately to a window.

"Jeremy," she said, "come here."

"Eh?" Her son looked alarmed. "Why should I?"

"Come here," she repeated. "What do you see?"

Jeremy approached his mother cautiously. "Well, of course I cannot see anything. It is the middle of the night, dash it."

"But if there were light, you would see the gardens and the riding track, and the courtyard and stables. And beyond that there are the woods, the pathway to the river." Jeremy nodded. "Supposing you woke up one morning and found that it had all disappeared?"

Jeremy said impatiently, "You're bamming me, Mama. That cannot happen."

"If Dracourt does not offer for Daphne that is exactly what will happen," Lady Larrimer said. "Without Dracourt, we are *lost.*"

Jeremy paled. "Surely it ain't that bad. There has to be another way."

"Lost," she repeated. "I know that Dracourt has little to recommend him but money, but he has a great deal of that. Do you have any 'blunt,' as you call it, Jeremy?"

In the complete silence that filled the room, Rosalys could hear the sigh of the April wind. Borne on the wind came Angus's quavered question and Dracourt's cheerful reply.

"Nay, lad, there's no need for you to be doing any of that. I'll manage champion. To bed with you. You look proper knackered."

"Do you have any money, Jeremy?" Lady Larrimer repeated. "Of course you do not. Rosalys will tell you that tonight we ate your papa's last stickpin. That is to say, not his stickpin, but the food bought through selling it." She placed her hands on her son's shoulders and looked him in the eye. "You must take your fences cleanly. We all must. Do you understand?"

Jeremy said nothing. "And you will not be rude to the viscount," Lady Larrimer continued. "His manners and ways may be peculiar, but he is our only hope."

Daphne burst into tears and threw herself into her sister's arms. Over her fair head Rosalys saw Jeremy's jaw clench. He looked precisely as Sir Henry had when he was wiped out on the 'Change.

Rosalys's forehead puckered into a worried frown. Jeremy was young and foolhardy. She would have to speak to him before he did something he might regret.

Rosalys, however, had little chance to get her brother alone. Jeremy seemed bent on avoiding his entire family. In fact, he spent much of the next few days away from Larrimer House in the company of Mr. Windwoode, who had condescended to teach him how to handle the ribbons. Rosalys, though understanding why her brother wanted to avoid Dracourt, was concerned. If Jeremy had to attach himself to someone, she wished that it had been Lord Edward.

Unfortunately, Lord Edward showed no sign of wanting to teach Jeremy how to drive a curricle or anything else. He was each day at Larrimer House, ostensibly to see his friend, to reminisce and ride with him, and often to have luncheon with the Larrimers. Whenever this happened,

Rosalys noted, Daphne took extra pains with her dress and toilette.

Jeremy did not come near his family again until Wednesday, when he was obliged to escort his sisters to the Montforts' meet. Mrs. Montfort had insisted on sending a chaise to convey the Larrimers to their estate, but this considerate gesture seemed to plunge the young man further into the dumps. He sat cracking his knuckles and glooming out of the window while Daphne prattled on happily.

"Indeed, the weather is quite perfect, and we are bound to have an excellent outing. How kind Mrs. Montfort was to invite us. Rosa, don't you think it is like old times?"

Jeremy glowered at his sister. "Gudgeon," he snorted. "The only good thing about the day is that that oaf Dracourt is waiting for Padgett and Windwoode instead of coming along with us. And it is not a *bit* like old times. We used to have our own carriage, then, and our own hunters, too. Dozens of them. My Lovell and your Mirrabelle, Rosa. Lord, to have them back."

"Well, you cannot," Daphne retorted petulantly. "And wishing does no good. I think you are the horridest boy to try and spoil the day for us because you have got the sulks."

Rosalys now said firmly that it would not do to break straws with each other over nothing. "Not about nothing," her brother exploded. "I would not expect a silly cabbage-head like Daphne to understand about horses, but *you* know! To think I'm obliged to borrow a nag from the colonel.

Probably a puffer," he added gloomily. "Odds are that it is touched in the wind."

But in this he did the colonel an injustice. In addition to some of the finest hounds in Dorset, Colonel Montfort maintained fourteen excellent hunters. Dressed in the scarlet coat of the Master of the Hunt, he greeted the Larrimers and reminisced about the good old days.

"Sir Henry and I raised a great deal of dust in the shires," he sighed. "Ah, those were the days, I can tell you. Now here," he added as a spanking gray was led out for Jeremy, "is a hunter you may approve of, young Jeremy. Nothing as good as you're used to, I'll be bound. Your father's stable was always above my touch."

Somewhat mollified, Jeremy sprang into the saddle and took the borrowed steed for a trial canter. "What an odious brat he is," Daphne murmured.

"It's hard for him." April wind tugged at Rosalys's knot of carefully coiled dark hair, and she lifted a hand to smooth it back. She understood what her brother was feeling, for when she thought of her mare, she could have wept.

Much as she enjoyed riding, she was glad that convention prevented her from having to accept the Montforts' kind offer of a horse. She liked the Montforts and knew their offer was well meant, but she could not bear to think of riding another man's horse. It was too much like taking charity.

"Oh," Daphne exclaimed excitedly, "they are here, Rosa."

Jeremy was cantering back across the green

fields that edged the Montforts' estate. Beside him rode Windwoode, while Dracourt and Lord Edward trotted behind on their horses.

"How well Lord Edward rides," Daphne murmured. "He is so graceful. Do you not think so, Rosa?"

"You like him, Daffy, don't you?"

Daphne smiled. "He is so kind and pleasant and so gentlemanly. Not like—well, not like you-know-who."

She broke off as the three men rode up. They saluted the colonel and bowed over his lady's hand. Each of them wore coats and top hats traditional to the hunt, but each wore his clothes differently. Lord Edward's coat fit him like a glove. Mr. Windwoode's white cravat had been tortured into the bulky mailcoach style. Dracourt's beautifully cut garments looked as if they had lost a struggle with their owner.

He strolled over to the ladies and shook Daphne's reluctant hand. "Fine day for the meet Miss Larrimer," he said cheerfully. "Nay, don't you and your sister look as fine as fi'pence!"

Looking pained at such gauche gallantry, Daphne tilted her pretty nose and walked pointedly away. Dracourt's eyes twinkled as he turned to Rosalys. "Was it summat I said?"

"I think you know very well."

"Me? I know nowt." He added, as Lord Edward hurried up to Daphne and bent swiftly over her hand, "I envy that Ned. He's a gallant soldier, a friend to count on, *and* he can kiss a lass's hand without having summat fall on his head. Now, that's a trick worth learning."

As she looked into his smiling blue eyes, the tightness around Rosalys's heart eased. "I wish you were riding with us today, lass," he was saying.

"I do not. It would not be the same, you see."

"I do see. You're missing that mare of yours."

Her fine brows drew together in a small frown. *"How* did you know about Mirrabelle?"

"Angus told me. He said that she was a high-stepper and that you were fond of her."

"I never knew Angus to be a prattle-box." An April breeze, richly scented with daffodils and meadow grass, belled out her cloak and danced a dark curl over her forehead. She pushed it back without much success. "Since he told you so much, he probably also said that all of Papa's horses were sold after he died."

Dracourt noted the angry glint in her eyes and knew that she was hurting. He wished that he had not spoken of her mare, and searched for something to give her comfort. Without thinking, he reached out to brush the vagrant curls away from her forehead and made a discovery: Her skin was like silk.

Drawing away from his touch, she looked at him uncertainly. "I beg you do not mention this subject in Jeremy's hearing. He feels badly enough without—"

She was interrupted by Mrs. Montfort bustling up to them. "I truly desire that you were riding with us, Miss Larrimer," the colonel's lady exclaimed, "but I quite agree with your dear mama that it would not be proper. I have instructed that comfortable seats be placed for you on that hillock. You will have a fine view from there. There will be some small refreshment for you in case time hangs heavy, and my abigail and a footman will attend your needs in everything. You and your sister need but ask for anything you desire."

As Rosalys thanked her hostess, Lord Edward exclaimed in impatient surprise, "Confound it, but my horse seems to have thrown a shoe."

The gentlemen gathered about Lord Edward's gray gelding. "Cannot think how it could have happened," Lord Edward continued. "Must have occurred on the way from Larrimer House. Awkward, this."

Colonel Montfort immediately placed his stable at Lord Edward's disposal, but Dracourt said, "I have a better notion. Ned, you've allus wanted to ride Gallant, haven't you? Now's your chance."

"Ride Gallant!" Lord Edward's eyes gleamed with excitement, but then he shook his head. "Couldn't do that, Drax. Dash it—couldn't think of it. What would you ride?"

"I do not intend to ride at all," Dracourt replied.

Colonel Montfort's eyes widened at this incredible news. "Not—ride?" he puffed.

"I feel uncommon lazy this morning, sir. Maybe it is the spring in the air. Any road, if the

ladies are willing. I will take my ease with them
on the hillock yonder."

Lord Edward protested feebly, but his eager-
ness to ride Gallant was so evident that he could
hardly keep his hands off the beautiful animal.
"He is complete to a shade, Drax," he exclaimed.
"I know there has never been a horse so well
schooled. It'd be a pleasure to ride him. Still,
seems shabby to leave you unhorsed."

Jeremy glanced at Windwoode. "Perhaps the
viscount *cannot* ride."

Rosalys rounded on him angrily. "Jeremy,
apologize at once."

"Drax was in the third dragoons," Lord Edward
added. "He was riding while you were in leading
strings, young Larrimer."

Dracourt interposed. "Nay, don't fratch your-
selves," he said mildly. "Sneck up, Ned, and
mount up, wilta?"

The other members of the hunt were already in
the saddle, and at the colonel's order, the huntsman and whippers-in had begun to cast for a fox
in a nearby covert. "My brother deserves to have
his ears boxed," Rosalys said to Dracourt. "I
apologize for him."

He smiled down at her. "As I told you before,
don't worry about things that don't matter."

The expression in his eyes unsettled, unbalanced her. It was as though he were looking not
at her but *into* her, as if he knew and understood
her thoughts. It was uncomfortable—but unac-
countably exciting.

Confused, she turned her eyes away. "Jeremy acts so badly because he is remembering how he and Papa rode to hounds," she explained. "They were mad for horses, both of them. When Papa's hunters were sold, Jeremy's heart was broken. If you could have seen him then, you would forgive his rudeness, perhaps."

He nodded sympathetically. "It must have been hell for you, too. Who arranged the sale?"

"Mr. Igramme, our solicitor, and Standish, who used to be father's chief groom." Dear Standish, who had loved and nurtured each horse that came into the Larrimer fold, who had stayed up with them when they were sick, and watched over every detail that went on in the stables. "It hurt Standish very much," she went on slowly, "but he found another position, I am glad to say, with one of Papa's friends. I hear he is doing famously."

"But he would come back in a minute if you were to call on him." She shook her head in doubt. "Any man would, Rosalys."

Before she could register the fact that he had called her by name, one of the hounds gave tongue. Others honored their leader's bay, and a high-pitched hulloa signaled the sighting of the fox.

Daphne hurried back to her sister's side. "There they go, Rosa. Isn't it exciting?"

"Perhaps we should climb the hillock as Mrs. Montfort meant us to do," Rosalys suggested.

Followed by Mrs. Montfort's stout, rosy-cheeked abigail and the footman, the three began to walk toward a nearby hillock.

"This is very fine," Daphne enthused.

The hillock was admirably suited for viewing the hunt, and Mrs. Montfort had seen to her guests' every comfort. A Turkish rug had been spread on the ground, and chairs and tables had been placed on it. The servants unpacked bottles of French wine, lemonade, thinly sliced ham, chicken, and beef. There were also small sugar cakes arranged on Sevres plates.

Dracourt grinned appreciatively at the feast but added, "Hasta no honest English ale, lad? I'm not one for Frenchy wine."

Daphne gave him a disgusted look and then pointedly turned her attention to the riders on the field. "How well he—they, I mean—ride," she murmured.

"Ned has reet good bottom," Dracourt agreed. Daphne blushed. "So does your brother."

Rosalys agreed. "Jeremy is fearless. He was on a horse before he could hardly walk."

"Only way to do it," Dracourt said. He heaped chicken and beef on his plate, adding, "It's the same as swimming. Learn while you're young. I wasn't able to crawl before my grandsire dropped me into the deepest part of our brook."

Daphne looked shocked and Rosalys said severely, "That is a whisker if I ever heard one, sir!"

"Nay, it's no lie. I were a toddler when he dropped me into the water and dragged me out again, half-drowned. But I learned to swim soon enough. And my name is Connor, not 'sir.' I should remind you of the penalty for that mistake, Miss Larrimer."

Rosalys directed a level gaze at him, decided that he was joking, and held her peace. Daphne sniffed.

"I'm a simple fellow," Dracourt confided, munching away. "It makes me break into hives—nay, into lumps the size of a robin's egg—when I'm sirrah-ed and my-lorded. I like plain speech."

He slurped his wine a little as he spoke. Daphne looked so horrified that Rosalys could hardly keep from laughing. But enough was enough.

"I think," she said, "that you are a humbug, and I—but, oh, look, I believe the fox has doubled back. They are riding this way."

Daphne bounced to her feet as the hounds bayed across the fields. Behind them streamed the master and huntsman followed closely by the others. All were riding with skill and speed, but Lord Edward outdid them all. He and Gallant seemed to move as one.

As he passed the hillock and the ladies, Lord Edward glanced in their direction. His eyes met Daphne's. Suddenly, however, his lordship's expression changed to one of surprise. He seemed to be uneasy in his saddle, to slide sideways. For a moment he fought to regain his seat but lost his battle and thudded to the ground.

Daphne screamed. "He will be trampled to death!"

"No, he will not," Rosalys cried. She had seen that Gallant had stopped short and had positioned himself so as to protect his rider from harm. Meanwhile, Dracourt was racing down the hillock toward his friend. In seconds he knelt by Lord Edward's side.

Daphne, dragging Rosalys with her, also began to run toward the field. "Dear Lord Edward, are you badly hurt?" she cried.

Hazel brown eyes in a pale face reassured her. "Sorry to have frightened you—assure you, in the pink," he said.

He attempted to rise but was pushed back by a large hand. "Stay still," Dracourt commanded. "You've had a bad fall, and I dislike the angle of that leg." He touched the limb, and Lord Edward winced and went pale. "The leg's broken, Ned."

Daphne began to cry. Rosalys suggested, "There is a doctor in the village."

"I'll go," Jeremy volunteered.

Rosalys saw that her brother and the other members of the hunt had ridden up. In the distance, she could hear the hounds being called off.

"I know where old Dr. Whittiwell can be found," Jeremy urged.

" 'Pon rep, it was a terrible accident." Mr. Windwoode looked almost as pale as Lord Edward. "We were riding neck and neck," he explained untruthfully, "and all of a sudden—never saw anything like it in my life. His saddle cinches must have burst."

Dracourt looked steadily at Windwoode. "So it would seem."

Mrs. Montfort was saying distractedly, "That such a thing could have happened—we'll carry him to our house."

"Wish to be no trouble—be up in a moment," gasped Lord Edward.

"Perhaps it were better to take him to Larrimer House," Rosalys interposed. "It is a little closer than your home, ma'am."

Though she addressed Mrs. Montfort, her eyes instinctively queried Dracourt, who nodded. "It's best to move him as little as possible. We'll make a litter and carry him to Larrimer House."

He turned to Jeremy. "Ride for the doctor, lad, and bring him back with you. Mrs. Montfort, if you could accompany the young ladies home? Her ladyship should be told what's happened. Sir," he added to the colonel, "you're no stranger to battlefield casualties. Perhaps you can help me make Ned more comfortable."

He spoke with such quiet authority that he was immediately obeyed. Jeremy cantered away, and the colonel dismounted to offer his aid. Mrs. Montfort put an arm around the frightened Daphne.

"Come, my dear, let the gentlemen attend to Lord Edward," she soothed. "We will drive to Larrimer House together in the chaise."

Unwillingly, Daphne allowed herself to be led away from the injured man's side. "It is that Dracourt's fault," she exclaimed bitterly to Rosalys. "If he had not offered poor Lord Edward his horse, this could not have happened."

"Fudge, Daffy!" Rosalys exclaimed indignantly. "How can you blame Connor—Dracourt, I mean—for an accident?" Then she stopped, more from surprise than because of Daphne's renewed tears. Since when, she wondered, had she become the viscount's champion?

Chapter Seven

Lady Larrimer faced the new crisis with her usual aplomb. By the time Dracourt carried his friend up the steps of Larrimer House, she had ordered the West Room made ready for his lordship. "For," she told the white-faced and apologetic Lord Edward, "it is highly unlikely that Dr. Whittiwell will wish you to be moved more than is absolutely necessary."

The doctor arrived soon after and proved her correct. Lord Edward's left leg was broken in two places, his back had sustained a bad sprain, and he had bruised his ribs. "Nonsense—feel the thing in an hour or so," his lordship protested feebly, but Dracourt bluntly told him not to be a slow-top.

"The doctor says as you're not to move, and that's what you'll do," he ordered. "Nay, lad," he added as his friend began to argue, "you'll not forget I'm your officer, and that's an order."

Lord Edward subsided. Lady Larrimer gave orders that Cook was to prepare broth for the invalid, and Daphne, hurrying upstairs with a bowl of barley water, whispered to Rosalys that she was *so* relieved.

"When I saw him lie so still I thought—but now the doctor assures us he only needs care and good nursing." Her eyes took on a warm glow as she added, "There *is* some truth in the saying that even a bad wind blows somebody some good."

In the days that followed, Rosalys was hard-pressed to discover what the good might be. True, Lord Edward was an ideal patient, making no demands and acting as cheerful as he possibly could. It was also true that when in the invalid's presence, Jeremy was not as rude to Dracourt and that Daphne, who read to Lord Edward and played backgammon with him to entertain him, had less time to contemplate her woes.

If only his lordship did not *eat*, Rosalys thought, as she faced Cook across an almost empty larder one morning. "You sees 'ow it is," the big woman said mournfully. "I can't feed the guests bread and water, Miss Rosa. Somefink 'as got to be done."

It was highly unpleasant, Rosalys mused, to be always thinking of food, but facts were facts. Not only did Lord Edward eat three meals a day, but so did his valet, Vraewick, who had naturally been moved to Larrimer House to attend his master during his convalescence. Now, the supply of foodstuffs was alarmingly low, and there were no more diamond stickpins to sell.

"Somefink 'as to be done," Cook repeated,

adding darkly, "Maybe we could kill one of them fowls."

In spite of her trouble, Rosalys smiled. "Hepzibah and Portia are as old as the hills and would be as tough as shoe leather," she said. "Besides, if we murder them, where would we get eggs?"

"There's that," Cook admitted.

"I collect that rabbit pie is one of your specialties," Rosalys continued. "Could you ask Tom to set traps in the meadows?"

"I 'ave asked 'im. Asked and asked. 'E promises, and then 'e doesn't do nofink. I'm very afeared, Miss Rosa, that Tom's up to mischief."

Rosalys, on her way out of the kitchen, turned to look at the big woman. Cook did not meet her eyes but smoothed suddenly trembling hands over her stiff-starched apron. " 'E doesn't come 'ome nights," she whispered. "Neighbors say as 'e's out to all hours. And—and 'e's secretive, like."

"Perhaps he has a sweetheart," Rosalys suggested.

Cook blew out her plump cheeks. "That one won't love nobody but 'imself. No, Miss Rosa, it's somefink else." She lowered her voice. "You heard as there is a riding horficer at the Royal George?"

Rosalys crossed the floor, captured Cook's hands in hers, and forced the big woman to meet her eyes. "Is Tom involved with the smugglers?" Cook shook her head, more in sorrow than in denial. "Then it *is* true about the tidesmen being active in Dorset."

"There's been smuggling done in these 'ere parts for many a year, but now with the war an' all, they've grown bolder. That's why I burned the meat the day as the viscount came to the 'ouse. Tom came 'urrying to the 'ouse, afraid as that the riding horficer would nab 'im."

Rosalys could think of little to say. She gave Cook's hands a sympathetic squeeze instead. "You have tried speaking with Tom?"

Cook's mouth twisted. "I'll save my breath to cool my porridge. No one can tell Tom anyfink. 'E'll be caught and transported or 'ung, that's all. I shouldn't care, but—but 'e's my dead sister's son, Miss Rosa. Blood is thicker than water."

Rosalys thought of this later as, bonneted and cloaked, she carried the market basket outside. No one saw her. Lord Edward had today managed to limp down to the morning room, and Daphne and Lady Larrimer were keeping him company. As for Jeremy, he was not in the house at all.

Yes, blood was thicker than water, and it was high time she had that talk with Jeremy. Sooner or later, he had to face facts. He could not forever escape reality by riding about with Mr. Windwoode. And besides, she needed his help.

Angus, his arms full of wood, met her on the steps of the house. "Did Tom Grady actually cut that stove wood for us?" Rosalys asked, astonished.

"No, ma'am, the viscount cut the wood. His

lordship assured me that he needed the exercise
and that he was exceedingly in my debt for allowing him to chop."

Angus would never permit himself to smile,
but Rosalys heard the warmth in the old man's
voice. Dracourt had certainly won the servants
over, she thought. "Have you seen Master Jeremy?" she asked.

"I believe that the young master is in the sta-
ble." Angus eyed her market basket sternly.
"Will he be accompanying you into the village,
Miss Rosa?"

"I am hoping that he will." But she was only
halfway to the stables when she saw her brother
leading his horse out of the stable door. She
called to him, but he did not hear her. Throwing
one long leg over the side of his horse, he cantered away toward the village.

"Of all the provoking young sap-skulls," she
exclaimed.

A cheerful "Good morning" interrupted her,
and she saw Dracourt at the stable door. He had
evidently been grooming his horse, for he was in
his shirtsleeves and was engaged in emptying a
pail of water on the ground.

"Is it a good morning?" she asked. Then she
added, "That odious boy. I wish I had thrown my
basket after him!"

"Nay, what good would that have done? His
horse'd have trampled it. A squashed basket's no
good to anyone."

It was on the tip of her tongue to retort irritably when her sense of humor rescued her. "Must you always be so sensible?" she sighed.

Dracourt shrugged broad shoulders. Then as Gallant whinnied from inside the stable, he added, "He hears your voice and wants to make his bow to you. Will you honor him with a visit?"

She hesitated. There were so many things that needed doing. But Gallant whinnied again, and their ancient cart horse answered back. The sound of the horses "talking" tugged at her memories. "Only for a moment," she agreed.

"Watch tha skirts," he commanded. Then, standing aside to let her pass he added, "Nay, but that's a fetching bonnet."

It was not in its first youth and was made of plain gray cloth, but she had added a feather that curled jauntily over the brim. No, Dracourt amended, the bonnet was not so much handsome as it was brave. That feather tossed its head and smiled at the world.

He watched Rosalys as she walked into the dimly lit stable. Her cloak may have been twice turned, but the hem of her much-used gown was bright with double trimming, and her step was brisk. Gallant, as if recognizing her mettle, bowed his stately head to her.

"You are such a beautiful fellow," she murmured, stroking him lovingly. "For fencing, for flying, or simply standing you are perfect, aren't you? It does me good to see you in these stables, sir, and so I tell you."

Dracourt watched her in silence. After a mo-

ment she looked at him over her shoulder and
arched her brows at his serious expression. "Do
not tell me that you have not heard Gallant
praised before," she said with a smile.

To her surprise, he did not return her smile.
"I'm wondering why you wanted your brother.
Happen you wanted him to go with you into the
village?"

"How did you—but of course. The market basket. Yes, I fancied he might accompany me, but it
is not important. And if you are going to offer to
escort me," she added quickly, "I assure you that
it is not necessary. The village is just a stone's
throw away."

His eyebrow arched quizzically and, recalling
the last time she had gone to market, she made
haste to change the subject. "Angus told me that
you have chopped our wood," she accused.

He grinned. "The old bubble was going out to
the woodpile with a skimble-skamble ax. He'd
have chopped his foot off, think on."

"Indeed I do 'think on.' I fear that you are a
hurly-burly fellow, sir." Then, seeing the quick
gleam in his eyes she added hastily, "I must be
gone."

"Tell me first why you came looking for your
brother. Summat is troubling you, lass."

The familiar little word did not offend her. Instead it conveyed a renewed sense of the strength
and kindness that she always seemed to find in
him. She smoothed Gallant's glossy neck and said
slowly, "You see, Jeremy is—so young."

"At heart he's a good lad," Dracourt reassured

her. "Look at how quick he rode down from Oxford to send me packing."

Troubled dark eyes looked up into his. "He's
full of fun and gig, but he's so heedless." Once
begun, the words poured out. "I collect that all he
cares for is riding about with Mr. Windwoode.
He *knows* how things are, but he doesn't seem to
care."

"As you say, he's young. Is that all that's
mithering you?" Dracourt asked.

He was very close to her. He had begun to
stroke Gallant absently, and his hand brushed
hers in passing. It was such a big hand, strong,
square, and capable that she did not think to pull
her own away.

"I wanted to talk to Jeremy about another matter. Do you remember what you told us about the
riding officer sent here to track down smugglers?"
He nodded. "Cook suspects that her nephew is
involved with the tidesmen."

"And you think Jeremy could have helped you
unravel that tangle? How?"

"Well, all of us used to play with Tom Grady as
children. We are in the country, you understand,
and even Mama relaxed her ideas about propriety
sometimes. We used to play hide-and-go-seek in
the woods." She paused. "I'm only a female, and I
doubt if Tom would have listened to me, but I'd
hoped that Jeremy could get him to give up this
business for Cook's sake."

Dracourt looked doubtful. "Jeremy's at an age
where he's toplofty. Happen he'd not thank you

for reminding him he had the village good-as-nowt as a playmate."

Her laugh was rueful. "I am persuaded that you are right. Jeremy is very much the gentleman these days. And yet he is so rag-mannered to you sometimes that I—well, I could box his ears for him. I cannot believe that you do not mind."

Something bright and blue blazed in his eyes for a moment. She tried to draw a bracing breath and caught, beyond the warm smells of horse and hay, the clean, vital fragrance of the man himself.

"No," he said, "I don't mind."

With an effort, Rosalys turned away from his blue gaze. "I must be going," she repeated.

"You're going to market now?" Some note in the deep voice made her look back at him. The disturbing light in his eyes had been replaced by concern. Suddenly, Rosalys wanted to rest her head on that broad shoulder.

Disturbed at this mad notion, she spoke defiantly. "Yes!"

"Now, don't be looking black and getting on your high ropes," he said, grinning. "Next thing you know, you'll be calling me 'sir' an' all. I only said what I did because I need your help. It's a delicate matter." She stared at him, surprised. "About Ned."

She blinked. "About Lord Edward?"

"Aye. He's poorly. He'd never admit to that, but that's why he had to sell out. He was three times wounded in the Peninsula and had a bad fever on the Portuguese border. It near carried

him off for good and all. Now, what with this
new hurt—well, you see how bad it could be."

Truly concerned, Rosalys exclaimed, "What
can we do?"

"Nowt—else Ned will realize that I've
squeaked beef on him. He's a devilish proud 'un.
But he needs special meals," Dracourt went on.
"He'd die before letting on, but he can't digest
what's good for other folk."

Rosalys's heart sank. "Special—meals?" she
asked faintly.

"If you'd consider letting me come wi' you to
the village—I'm asking a lot, but then, a big gowk
like me doesn't know the first thing about buying
for invalids. Happen you could advise me what to
buy." She started to speak, and he held up a big
hand. "I've my pride, too."

Bewildered, she said, "I do not understand."

"I mean that it is my fault that Ned took hurt.
It *were* my horse he were riding. And here he's
been foisted on you, as don't know him from
Adam, and here I've been standing by wanting to
help and not daring to for fear of insulting your
lady mother. Which is a prospect that no man is
brave enough to face." He paused. "But if you
don't tell anyone that *I* mean to buy Ned the vict-
uals he needs, nobody'd be the wiser. Do you
see?"

She was beginning to see very well. As usual,
Dracourt made perfect sense. And it was as if the
sun had suddenly burst into the sky. She envi-
sioned chops and hasty mutton and rack of lamb,
fowls roasted on the spit, fresh brook trout. She

thought of Cook's face when she saw viands in
the larder again.

"Well, will ye do it, Miss Rosa?" Dracourt
asked anxiously.

"I think I might be persuaded," she said. And
then, unable to dissemble, she smiled sunnily at
him. "And of course you knew that, didn't you?
You are the most complete hand, Connor St. Cyr.
Have I told you so?"

His eyes kindled. "You have an' all."

It took only a few moments for Connor to
wash and don his coat, and in that time Rosalys
privately explained to her mother that the viscount needed help in buying certain delicacies for
his friend. Lady Larrimer looked thoughtful.

"You might try to discover how the wind sits,"
she said. "It would be helpful to know what he
thinks of Daphne. I have not forced the issue,
hoping that they would get to know each other
first."

Rosalys said she would do her best, but as they
walked down the pathway she was intent on putting together a mental shopping list. Suddenly,
she checked herself. Suppose Lord Edward could
not digest these precious things?

"What can your friend safely eat?" she asked
Dracourt.

"I leave that to you. I know he's partial to beef
and kidney pie, and cream with his pudding, and
a rack of lamb might be welcome," was the answer.

"What a sensible invalid," Rosalys approved.

She felt a sense of power as she swept into Jason's butcher shop this time. Sensing the change in Miss Larrimer, Jason gaped at the big fair-haired man behind her and hastily filled her order—which, because of Dracourt's constant urgings and additions, soon grew enormous. Jason then gaped some more as the big gentleman placed gold sovereigns on the counter and ordered the entire order sent around promptly to Larrimer House. The butcher ended by bowing so many times that Rosalys was sure he would split himself in two before they got clear of the shop.

Once outside, Connor drew a sigh of relief. "That's a load off my mind," he exclaimed. "Miss Rosa, I don't know what I would have done without you."

There was nothing but heartfelt gratitude in his voice, but suspicion had begun to grow in her mind. "Naturally you bought that mountain of food for Lord Edward," she murmured.

He gave her an innocent look. "Of course I did. A man who does not look after his friends is a very poor fish."

They had approached the Royal George as they spoke, and Rosalys recognized the pair of grays hitched to a familiar curricle. Holding the horses' bridle was Tom Grady.

Seeing her, he touched the brim of his cap. What should have been a respectful gesture was spoiled by the insolent look of appraisal that he gave her. "Miss Larrimer," he drawled.

As he spoke, the inn door opened, and the Honorable Aubrey Windwoode appeared. He was dressed in the kick of fashion in a coat with a multitude of capes, a white waistcoat that tried valiantly to nip in his waist, nut brown pantaloons, and Hessians so polished they reflected the sun. His hair had been arranged carefully à la Titus, and the points of his collar were so high that they nearly eclipsed his face.

"Oh, good heavens," Rosalys murmured. "He has seen us."

Windwoode, who had put his quizzing glass to his eye, now let it fall. With a gesture of supreme condescension, he strolled down the stone steps toward Rosalys and Dracourt, who declared, "Tha's decked out in fine style, lad. Fair puts me in the shade."

Windwoode acknowledged this compliment as his due and bowed over Rosalys's hand. She felt revolted at the touch of his moist lips on her skin and was even more disgusted when Windwoode said, "I could wish you a better place in which to take the air. God, what a filthy little village this is."

As he waved a perfumed handkerchief, Jeremy came out of the Royal George. Rosalys saw that her brother was unconsciously aping the older man's mincing steps. He looked somewhat embarrassed when he saw her, but his face hardened at the sight of her companion.

"Hulloa, Rosa," he called. "Isn't it famous? Mr. Windwoode's going to teach me how to turn a corner in style." Then, deliberately ignoring Dracourt, he added, "Can we go now, Windwoode? 'Pon rep, it looks as if it may rain."

Windwoode grinned with odious familiarity. "The bantling thinks he's a top sawyer already. Servant, Miss Larrimer. Er, Dracourt."

Rosalys watched unhappily as her brother took his place in the older man's curricle. Jeremy then said something to Tom Grady, who touched his cap eagerly.

"Well," Dracourt commented, "happen I was wrong. Your brother and Grady are on good terms, I see. I think I will have a word with yon lad."

He took two strides away from Rosalys's side, and clamped a large hand down on Grady's shoulder.

Grady started. " 'Ere, what's the matter?" he demanded truculently. "You take your mitts off me, see?"

"Easy, lad. No need to fatch thyself." Dracourt lowered his voice so that Rosalys could not hear what he said, but she could and did watch the various changes of expression on Tom Grady's face. Cook's nephew began by looking angry, then resentful, and then quite frightened. When, after a minute or two Dracourt let him go, he bowed to her in a highly respectful, if agitated, way.

"M-miss Larrimer," he stammered. "My auntie says that you m-might be needing me at the house."

Astonished, Rosalys could only nod.

"I'll be there," Tom then said and made a hasty retreat.

"What did you say to him?" Rosalys marveled.

"Nowt as makes any difference."

"I doubt *that*," she sighed. "It must be fine to be as big as you and inspire fear in people."

He chuckled. "Warn't me that afeared that gormless lad. Look over there."

Rosalys followed Dracourt's nod and saw that some horsemen had just ridden up to the inn. Their leader was a small fellow enveloped in a heavy dark coat. He looked harmless enough. "Yon's Merchum, the riding officer that has our Tom in a quake."

The little man was looking about him, and his eyes now rested on her. Rosalys felt herself watched, weighed, and dismissed all in one second. No wonder Tom had taken to his heels, she thought. The riding officer was definitely no fool.

Dracourt's hand at her elbow gently urged her onward. As they walked he said, "If you have trouble with Grady again, tell me. I've dealt with lads like him before. They need a strong hand on their shoulder from time to time."

"Jeremy would profit from such a hand," she sighed. "Not from you, of course. *That* he would not stand for."

"Aye," he agreed, "but I mind what you say. It goes against my grain, too, to see him bosom-bows with Windwoode. I don't trust the man."

"No more do I," she said. "You know I loathe him."

Connor's fine mouth tightened. "He realizes that if he bothers you again in any way he'll get the hiding of his life. No, he'll keep his distance. It's not that I meant."

Surprised at the change in his voice, she stared up at him. "What, then?"

"My saddle cinches did not break," he told her bluntly. "They were cut."

"Cut!" Her eyes widened with astonishment, then with horrified understanding. "You think Mr. Windwoode did it?"

"I waited for Ned that morning, if you remember. Windwoode rode up with him, and they both came into the stable with me. Ned desired to consult me about his horse, so I went outside with him. Windwoode remained behind—with Gallant." Connor paused. "He had the time and the opportunity. As for motive—"

She remembered Mr. Windwoode sitting in the mud. She recalled his look of pure hate that day at Larrimer House. "But—it is infamous. You could have been killed." She had a fleeting image of Dracourt's powerful body being thrown from his galloping horse and lying mangled on the grass. "I wonder that you could keep from strangling the little beast," she cried, sickened.

"I cannot prove anything, but this I will say. I would no more want a brother of mine with that fribble than I would want him lying down with venomous snakes. You have influence with Jeremy. Talk to him."

"If he will listen. But you must know that he is flattered that an older man, a top sawyer and a gentleman of the ton, is paying attention to him.

Already he apes Windwoode's manners."
Rosalys's forehead puckered thoughtfully as she
added, "The question is, *why* is Windwoode being
so friendly to a mere 'bantling,' as he puts it?"

Dracourt was silent. After a moment Rosalys
said, "Jeremy still thinks like a rich man's son. It
was a blow to him when Papa lost his fortune. Of
course, we suffered, too, but Jeremy was just a
child. It was hardest for him, I think."

"What of you?" he wondered. "What were
you about when the world fell apart?"

She smiled. "I had just had my come-out. My
grandaunt, the Marchioness of Lakefield, was one
of my sponsors at Almack's." She gave a rueful
chuckle. "Actually, I don't know if my fate
would have been very different had Papa not lost
his fortune. I didn't *take,* you see."

"I find that hard to believe."

She said frankly, "But it is true. There were a
few gentlemen who attended me, but they were
probably in the market for a rich wife. The sad
truth is that as soon as Papa's fortune disappeared, so did they."

Dracourt thought several unprintable things
about Rosalys's fickle suitors but contented himself by saying that she was better off without *that*
sort. Rosalys nodded and said she thought so,
too.

"You must not think that I mind. My pride was
hurt, I grant you, but it would have been much
worse had my engagement been printed in the
papers—or, even more horrible, if I had been
married to someone who only wanted Papa's for-

tune. But," she said wistfully, "Mama says that is the way of the world."

They had come clear of the village and were near the path that led to Larrimer House. From this point they could see the long, silver curve of the Stour River as it wound through field and down and meadowland toward the sea. "It is ludicrous, is it not?" she asked slowly. "Everyone wants money. Some people work for it and some become highwaymen or smugglers. Meanwhile, our friends in the Polite World marry for it."

She broke off, suddenly, remembering the reason for Dracourt's presence at Larrimer House. Guiltily, she recalled Lady Larrimer's instructions.

"At any rate," she said rather hastily, "I was left on the shelf. My grandaunt, Lady Lakefield, was quite out of charity with me."

"I can't think why." Dracourt stopped walking and faced her. "I would have thought she could see the truth."

"And what, pray, is that?"

"You are worth a hundred of those insipid debs," Dracourt said firmly. "Any man with his wits about him would know that, Rosalys."

He took her hand in his and bowed over it. In spite of the April cool, her cheeks felt warm. When she drew her hand away, there was a warmth where his lips had rested moments ago. Unconsciously, Rosalys clasped her hands together as if to preserve that warmth.

"You forget yourself," she murmured.

He looked at her quizzically. "I am sorry if plain speaking offends you, but it is God's truth."

She shook her head. "I did not mean that. What I meant was—do you realize that you have forgotten to speak broad Yorkshire for several minutes?"

Chapter Eight

Dracourt looked startled for a moment, but he rallied almost immediately. "Supposing I told you that Ned has had me practicing to speak like a park-saunterer?"

"Fustian!"

He gave a deep sigh. "You are a hard woman."

"For some time I have suspected that you were hoaxing us."

"Nay!" he exclaimed so ingenuously that she could not hold back a chuckle. Then, shaking his head, he offered her his arm. "I must apologize for all the furniture I upset. And the flower vases, too. It made extra work for you, I realize. I must find some way of repaying you."

"You already have repaid us! Only think of chopping wood for Angus, and carrying coal scuttles upstairs. To say nothing of bringing in pails of water for Cook. She told me this morning—"

"That doesn't signify," he interrupted rather hastily. "I owe you an explanation as to why I have been acting the part of the country clown."

"Kedwell's letter, wasn't it?"

"That confounded letter!" He looked quite grim suddenly. "Damn my father and his ridiculous notions of friendship."

"Is there no way of getting clear of it?" she asked anxiously.

"None that I know of. Your mother wrote out a copy of the letter and sent it to me in Yorkshire. I showed it to my solicitor."

"And he said?"

"That I was in the basket," Dracourt said bluntly.

Rosalys hesitated, then asked, "I collect, then, that you don't have a tendre for my sister?"

"You might as well ask *her* that."

"Poor Daffy—you have her in a quake. She truly wishes you in Jericho." Rosalys added thoughtfully, "No, of course you would *not* suit. That is why you chose to try and get Mama to cry off."

"Aye, I did an' all."

"You did it very well. You convinced everyone, even the servants, though they like you very well in spite of your rustic manners."

"But I did not convince you?"

"You said it yourself; you cannot make a sow's ear out of a silk purse," she said.

His eyes kindled but he only asked soberly, "How sits the wind with Lady Larrimer?"

"Unfortunately, Mama is holding to her guns."

"There is no hope she'll give it up?"

"Mama is a proud woman," Rosalys began, "and she was truly horrified when you arrived. You made such a cake of yourself that I believe that if Lord Edward hadn't come when he did, she *might* have torn up Kedwell's letter. But when she saw that your friend so obviously admired you, she took heart that he could—well, make you acceptable."

"Poor Ned," Dracourt said ruefully. "When he saw me tripping over chairs, and falling over my own feet, he was certain I'd turned Bedlamite. There was no way I could explain—then." He saw Rosalys's expression and added gently, "I had to tell him, you know."

She withdrew her hand from his arm and turned away. *"What* he must think of us!"

Dracourt took her hands in his and drew her around to face him. "Ned would never betray a confidence, lass."

"Even so—and pray do not," she cried, "call me 'lass.' It is quite improper as you well know, especially since you are no longer playing the part of a—a—"

"Nodcock?" he suggested helpfully. "Puff-headed block? Good-as-nowt whopstraw?"

Her severe stare was spoiled by the twinkle in her eyes and the fact that the corners of her lips kept twitching suspiciously. "You are much worse than any of those things," she lectured, "and if the matter were not so serious, I would give you the set-down you deserve. But, oh," Rosalys sighed, "Mama has landed us in such a

mare's nest. Even if you were willing to offer for
Daphne, our troubles wouldn't be over. Everyone
would say that it was cream-pot love and that the
Larrimers were forced to dangle after a wealthy
husband."

"A terrible business," he agreed somberly, but
Rosalys saw the irrepressible glint in his eyes.

"I understand what you would say. It is very
odious for you, too. In your position, I do not
know what I would have done."

"No?" Dracourt spoke with some difficulty. He
was fighting a growing impulse to gather her into
his arms. Rosalys Larrimer, he thought somewhat
hazily, was like wine. Wine—or perhaps the pure
air at the top of a mountain. She could dizzy a
man and make him lose all sense of reason.

Words rushed to his lips. They were words that
had begun to form in his heart that evening when
she helped him tie his wretched cravat. Since
then his feelings had grown richer and clearer.

She looked so troubled now as she stood with
her slender hands still in his and the sunlight
shining down on her raised face that he almost
blurted out all his thoughts. Almost—

Dracourt stopped himself. *Not now.* Now while
that damned letter was still in the way.

He let go of her hands and folded his own behind his back. "We can be allies," he suggested.

Surprised at the abrupt change in his manner,
she looked at him uncertainly. "I do not know
what you mean."

"I mean that we want the same thing. Perhaps
you can persuade your mother to destroy

Kedwell's letter. Then our troubles would be over."

She nodded thoughtfully. "I will do my best to help you, but if Mama is *determined* to make the match there is little anyone can do. No one has ever changed her mind."

They had started to walk again. "I understand her position. Her family is beside the bridge."

His tone was dry, and she felt her pride stiffen. "You must not concern yourself about that," she said sternly. "The Larrimers are most certainly not your problem. Besides, *your* position is desperate enough."

She had no idea, he thought ruefully, just how desperate it was. "I can see the thing I want to do, but not how to accomplish it," he admitted, then added, "I tell thee, lass, I'm fair flummoxed."

He was trying to make light of an intolerable situation. Gamely, she met him halfway. "I'll help thee if I can, lad," she improvised, "but it may not be enough."

"If we work together, that'll be champion. Eh, you're a goodly lass."

She glanced up at him. Her rosy-lipped half smile and the suddenly merry look in her eyes were irresistible. Dracourt caught his breath. Next moment he'd stopped walking, and his big hands went to her shoulders.

Finding herself turned gently to face him, Rosalys felt light-headed. When he bent his fair head, her own tipped back. Dark eyelashes fluttered down to veil her eyes.

Their kiss was a mere brush of the lips. But in

that heart's beat of time, Rosalys felt as if her whole world had turned inside out. She was no longer sure whether she was standing on the ground or flying through the air.

Momentarily, then, he took his lips away. She caught a glimpse of his face, saw the blue fire in his eyes, the tender curve of his mouth. It seemed as if everything in creation was waiting.

Then he kissed her again, and there was nothing light or diffident about this kiss. His lips claimed hers with a single-minded passion. Reason and conscious thought fell before that onslaught, and she tasted the sweetness of his mouth and tongue, felt the unfamiliar roughness of his cheek.

Then, suddenly, his lips left hers. His arms unwound themselves, and he stepped away with such abruptness that she nearly fell forward.

"Now *that*," Dracourt exclaimed, "is the proper way to seal our bargain."

"B-bargain?"

"In Yorkshire, we seal bargains with a kiss."

His deep voice sounded matter-of-fact, but his smile was a little sheepish. "Perhaps it was not exactly the thing, but we were talking dialect and I forgot propriety in the spirit of the moment."

"The spirit of the moment," she repeated. Her heart was beating hard, and her breathing hadn't yet returned to normal. Suddenly she wished it was permissible to box the Viscount Dracourt's noble ears.

"I beg your pardon if I offended you," he said

cheerfully. "After all, I would not want to start
out our partnership by breaking straws."

Rosalys tried her level best to sneer. It was not
a success. "I beg you will not make refine on it,"
she said icily, "but I should tell you that I detest
country manners."

A kiss to seal a bargain. That was all it had
meant. It was only a childish country custom.
What else would it have been, widgeon? she demanded of herself.

"They will worry about us if we are gone too
long," she said haughtily. "I will do my best to
persuade Mama. I hope that she will listen."

Dracourt was suddenly grim. "She had better."

The remainder of the walk homeward was ac-
complished in silence. As they came past the
woods and through the side gate, they saw a trim
landaulet standing in the courtyard.

"That is Mr. Igramme's—our solicitor's—landaulet," Rosalys exclaimed. "I wonder what
brings him here?"

She asked the same question of Angus when he
opened the door for them. "I am not sure,
ma'am," the old butler said. "Mr. Igramme has
been with my lady in the drawing room for some
time. Her ladyship commanded me to see that
they were not disturbed."

With growing apprehension Rosalys glanced
upward at the first floor and at the closed drawing room door. "Has Master Jeremy returned?"

Angus said he had not. "Miss Daphne is, I believe, reading to Lord Edward in the morning

room. And the butcher's boy has arrived, ma'am. Cook begs that you go down to the kitchen when you have a moment."

When Rosalys had promised to do so, Angus said to Dracourt, "My lord, Tom Grady has come from the village. He makes bold to see your lordship."

"Where is he?"

"He is engaged in cleaning the stables, my lord."

Rosalys's attention was diverted from the solicitor's visit. "Angus, you are funning us! Do you mean to tell me that *Tom Grady* is cleaning our stables?"

"Difficult as it is to believe, Miss Rosa, he has been hard at work since he arrived a half hour ago."

Dracourt grinned at Rosalys's astonished expression. "I'll go see t'lad now," he said and strode off toward the stable. Rosalys stared after him.

"It is vur-ry odd indeed, ma'am," Angus burred. "Cook feels certain it is the miracle she has prayed for."

More likely Tom had benefited from the rough edge of Dracourt's tongue, but Cook was not to know this. Rosalys could hear the big woman singing hymns of thanksgiving in the kitchen. "I'll see her as soon as I change," she told Angus.

She climbed the stairs to the first floor of the house and paused there to listen. All was quiet except for the murmur of voices from the drawing room. Though she could not make out anything that was said, she thought she detected agitation in her mother's voice.

Perhaps Daphne could tell her why Igramme had come. Lost in that thought, Rosalys did not at first realize how quiet the morning room was. When she had reached the door, however, she hesitated. Perhaps Lord Edward has fallen asleep?

She gave the half-open door a little push and glanced inside. She then saw that Lord Edward was far from asleep. He was sitting up on the daybed and holding Daphne in his arms. He was kissing her, and Daphne was kissing him back. "Darling, my darling," Lord Edward was murmuring between kisses.

For a moment Rosalys stood frozen in the doorway. Then, holding her skirts tightly to keep them from rustling, she backed into the hallway. Should she go away? But if she did, perhaps Angus would walk by the morning room and see the lovers.

"That would never do," she murmured.

She waited a few moments and then, humming a song, approached the morning room as noisily as possible. Her ruse was successful, for by the time she reached the door, Lord Edward was deeply engrossed in the newspaper while Daphne, her cheeks very pink, was sewing industriously.

Lord Edward looked up from his paper—held upside down, Rosalys noticed—at her greeting. "Back from your walk already, Miss Larrimer? Always believed April walks were invigorating."

"You are right, but it is still quite cool outside.

It is much more pleasant in this room." She turned to Daphne. "Has Mr. Igramme been here long, Daffy?"

"Yes, for *ages*," Daphne fluttered. "Mama was sitting with us and then Mr. Igramme came, but he insisted on speaking with her in private. That is all I know." Her pink cheeks grew crimson. "Ed —Lord Edward and I have been wondering what they could be talking about for so long."

Rosalys wondered, too. Concealing her uneasiness, she said briskly, "Well, I must change for luncheon. Will you be able to come to luncheon today, Lord Edward?"

"If this nursing angel says I'm to come, I will come." He sent Daphne a worshipful look. "Never been looked after so well. Too kind. Too good by half."

"Oh, my lord, you will *quite* turn my head." Daphne gave his lordship her most entrancing smile. "Who would not do everything possible for such a patient?"

Rosalys was beginning to feel definitely de trop in the room. She also knew that if she left them unchaperoned, the scene upon which she had stumbled was likely to be repeated.

"Will you come upstairs with me, Daffy?" she asked. "I need to ask your advice."

Daphne rose reluctantly and followed her sister into the hall. "What is it, Rosa?" she demanded.

"I would rather tell you in private, dear. Let us go to my room." Daphne glanced back at the morning room. "I'm persuaded that no horrible fate will befall Lord Edward while you are gone."

"He is our *guest* after all," Daphne murmured. As she followed her sister up the stairs she added, "Mama said I must do my best to make the time pass pleasantly for him."

"I am sure that you do your best," Rosalys soothed.

"I always try to obey Mama," Daphne said virtuously. "But tell me, how was *your* morning, Rosa? It must have been tedious with *that man* as your only companion."

Rosalys's murmur was indistinct.

"If Dracourt comes anywhere near me, I feel the need to scream," Daphne went on. "I am always in a tweak that he will upset something in my lap or tear my dress or make a cake of himself. I cannot credit why dear Lord Edward likes him."

"Ah," Rosalys said feebly.

"They say birds of a feather flock together, but Dracourt is a—a big crow, and Lord Edward is a swan. He is so graceful and gentlemanly and so *fine.*"

Suddenly, Daphne caught her sister's hands. "Rosa, please help me. You are so clever, and Mama doesn't browbeat you the way she does me. I don't want to marry Dracourt. You see, I—"

"You have formed a tendre for someone else, perhaps," Rosalys suggested.

"How did you know? But, yes, you are right. Rosa, I love another."

She sounded so dramatic that Rosalys couldn't help smiling. "Lord Edward is all that is noble and good," Daphne went on rapturously.

Opening the door to her room, Rosalys drew Daphne inside. Taking her sister's hands in hers, she looked deep into those lovely amethyst eyes. "Has Lord Edward asked you to marry him?"

"N-no. But he loves me." Daphne tossed her blond curls defiantly. "He has said so. And—and he has kissed me, and I have kissed him back. If Dracourt had suggested such a thing, I should have screamed and slapped his face. It would have been like kissing a toad."

Before Rosalys could respond to this, Angus coughed at the door. "Mr. Igramme is about to take his departure, ma'am," he announced.

"Does Mama wish me to come down?" Rosalys asked. The old man hesitated.

"That was not *precisely* what her ladyship ordered. But I thought—" He broke off, but his expression spoke volumes.

"Yes, we need to know what has taken place," Rosalys agreed. "I will come down immediately."

"I shall go downstairs also," Daphne announced. "Lord Edward has been alone too long."

Rosalys cast about for something that would keep Daphne from Lord Edward's side until she could chaperon these too-eager lovers. "Daffy, I have meant to tell you. That hair ribbon is not *precisely* the same shade as your dress. I collect you put it on by mistake this morning."

Daphne immediately flew to look in the glass. Sure that her sister would now be occupied for some time, Rosalys followed Angus into the hall. She was hastening down the steps when she saw the solicitor come out of the drawing room. One

look at his thin, scholarly countenance and her
heart sank.

Mr. Igramme had brought them bad tidings before, but he had never looked as haggard as he
did now. She had meant to ask him what was
happening, but now she hesitated, afraid. *I don't
want to know,* Rosalys mused.

As if he'd heard that cowardly thought, the solicitor glanced up and saw her on the stairs. "Miss
Larrimer." He bowed.

She curtsied and asked as steadily as she could,
"You have come to see Mama about the entail?"
He nodded. "It is so bad?" she whispered.

"Sir Henry's creditors are giving her ladyship
two weeks to pay the mortgage."

"Two wee—but, Mr. Igramme, there is no possible way that this could be managed. Are they
Bedlamites that they demand such a thing?"

"They are businessmen, ma'am." Mr. Igramme's nostrils flared in cold contempt. "They smell
of the shop. They care little as long as they can
count their profit. They have been silent this
while not from kindness but because they felt
sure that a profitable marriage was about to be
arranged between your sister and the Viscount
Dracourt."

Did everyone know about that wretched letter?
"But now?" she prompted.

"Now the creditors feel that such a match may
not be forthcoming. They want matters settled at
once. There is nothing I can do to stave them off
unless an engagement is announced immediately."

Thanking him through suddenly dry lips, Rosalys watched the solicitor take his leave. Then, reluctantly, she knocked on the drawing room door and went inside.

Lady Larrimer was sitting in a chair with her head in her hands. She looked up sharply, saw that it was Rosalys, and said, "Close the door, if you please." Rosalys obeyed. "Has Igramme gone?"

Rosalys nodded. "I know why he came, Mama."

"Then there is no need to explain. Has Dracourt returned to the house?"

Rosalys thought of the way Lord Edward and Daphne had looked at each other. She recalled her promise to Dracourt. "I must speak with you," she said firmly.

"Later, Rosalys. You must realize," the Dowager Lady Larrimer added dryly, "that this is no time for a cose. I have other business to attend to."

Rosalys took some steps into the room. "I beg you will listen to me first, ma'am."

Lady Larrimer started to shake her head, but the determined look in her daughter's eyes made her pause. "What flummery is this?" she demanded sternly.

"No flummery. I won't take much of your time, I promise."

With none too good a grace her ladyship said, "Well?"

"You asked me to find out how the wind sits with Con—with Dracourt. He has no desire to

marry Daphne, and she loathes him." Deliberately blunt, Rosalys noted the narrowing of her
mother's eyes. "It is infamous to hold Kedwell's
promise over Dracourt's head. To marry those
two would bring nothing but tragedy."

A struggle was taking place in Lady Larrimer's
heart. Rosalys could almost see the battle between her love of Larrimer House and her horror
of the bungling viscount. For a moment, Rosalys
hoped that ancestral pride might tip the balance
and force her mother to cry off, but her ladyship
shook her head.

"It cannot be helped. An engagement is the
only thing that will satisfy those vultures."

Rosalys took the bull by the horns. "Mama,
someone else has a tendre for Daphne."

"Lord Edward. I am not blind, miss," her ladyship said, "nor yet in my dotage. Those two have
smelled of April and May for some time. But
Lord Edward is an honorable man. I knew he
would not speak out of turn and offer for his
friend's affianced bride."

But that had not prevented him from falling in
love. "If Kedwell's letter was destroyed," Rosalys
argued, "everything would be different. Surely,
Lord Edward is a much more acceptable son-in-
law? Daphne and he love each other. They would
suit so well."

Lady Larrimer sighed. "He is not as rich as
Dracourt."

"How do you know?"

"Igramme made some inquiries for me. Lord

Edward has a decent living, but his estate is encumbered. Larrimer House must be *safe.*"

Rosalys crossed the room, sank down before her mother, and clasped both of the older woman's icy hands in hers. "Mama, Lord Edward may not be as wealthy as the viscount, but he would not allow Larrimer House to be sold off to those odious men. He would offer for Daphne the moment you tore up Kedwell's letter. Please, let those two young people be happy."

Lady Larrimer suddenly looked her years. "Have you considered this, Rosa? Daphne is a nonpareil, and Lord Edward is housebound with time on his hands. It could be calf love with him. He may not declare himself. And if I tore up the duke's letter, what hold would I have on Dracourt?"

There was a silence in which the outer door opened, and Dracourt's deep voice echoed up the hall. Lady Larrimer met her daughter's eyes for a speaking moment. "Have the goodness to fetch the viscount," she said.

Very slowly Rosalys went down the hall. Her steps dragged even more as she approached the morning room. She could hear Dracourt talking cheerfully to his friend, and the realization that she had tried to help him and failed wore heavily on her heart. *How will I tell him?* she wondered.

As the thought touched her mind, he came out of the morning room and saw her. His eyes lit up at the sight of her but narrowed warily as she said, "Mama begs that you see her in the drawing room."

She could sense the tensing of his big body, but his voice remained calm. "Now?"

"Yes, I am afraid so."

It did not take long to cross the hall. "Mama, here is Lord Dracourt," Rosalys announced. She would gave gone away then, but Lady, Larrimer stopped her.

"Stay, Rosa. You are the eldest of my children and should be present. Lord Dracourt, will you sit?"

"I'll stand, ma'am," he answered stolidly.

"You know why I invited you here."

"I have a good notion."

He spoke so coldly that even Lady Larrimer was daunted. She seemed to be having trouble meeting his hard, blue stare. "A bargain is a bargain," she began somewhat uneasily. "Your father, the Duke of Kedwell, and my late husband made an agreement. The question, sir, is what do you intend to do about it?"

Trapped, Dracourt thought. He looked at the pale oval of Rosalys's face and then at her mother's determined one. "Perhaps you should tell me," he said unhelpfully.

Lady Larrimer shot to her feet. "Oh, let's have done with this flummery," she cried. "I do not wish to peel eggs with you. I ask you to your head, sir, will you offer for my daughter, or are you going to try and cry off?"

Rosalys watched several emotions flicker across Dracourt's face, but he remained stone-still.

"Because if you intend to cry off," her ladyship

warned, "I will personally make sure that the world realizes you are a skirter."

"Mama!"

"That you are a loose-screw and a counter-coxcomb," her ladyship continued heatedly. "A yawl-rigged whipper snapper!"

"Oh, I say—that's doing it too brown, ma'am!"

Jeremy was standing in the half-open drawing room doorway. He did not try to hide his glee at hearing Dracourt being given a thundering scold. "I could hear you all the way to the stables." He grinned. "It's bad form to let the servants hear you brangling."

"Jeremy," Rosalys hissed, "go *away.*"

"Take a damper," Jeremy retorted.

Aware that her offspring's appearance had taken some of the wind out of her sails, her ladyship nevertheless squared up at the viscount. "Sir, I await your answer. Do you or do you not mean to offer for my daughter?"

"Offer for—well, 'pon rep, that's the outside of enough," Jeremy cried. "Look, why are you coaxing him for? Why get into a pucker if he don't offer for Daffy? Who needs him?"

"Silence!" Lady Larrimer roared. "Jeremy, you will go to your room immediately. I will not tolerate your hurly-burly ways."

"*My* hurly-burly ways? Well, I like that, when you're the one who started this argle-bargle," Jeremy retorted.

As mother and son eyed each other like duelists about to engage, Dracourt rapped out: "Yes!"

There was immediate silence. Lady Larrimer and Jeremy stopped glaring at each other and stared at Dracourt instead.

"Yes?" her ladyship repeated. After a long pause she added cautiously, "Do you mean that you intend to offer for my daughter?"

"That is what I intend to do," Dracourt agreed calmly.

Rosalys hadn't known she was holding her breath. Now she let it out in a sigh.

No one heard her, for Jeremy had slammed his fist against the door. "You will regret this, Mama," he cried. "Whatever happens now, it's—it's going to be on your head."

He stormed out of the room. A moment later, the outer door slammed behind him. Lady Larrimer winced at the sound. "Detestable child," she muttered. Then she turned her gaze to the equally detestable but very necessary viscount. "I can then conclude that you will become formally affianced to my daughter?" she asked coldly.

With his eyes on Rosalys's face, Dracourt repeated, "Yes."

"All the forms must be observed. A notice of your engagement will be placed in the *Morning Post,* but before this, you must meet the family. I shall arrange a gathering of the family at the earliest opportunity." Lady Larrimer began to smile triumphantly. "I will invite Aunt Lakefield to Larrimer House. I will invite all of them!"

Rosalys could bear no more. "You will not need me anymore, Mama," she murmured.

She found it hard to speak. There was a heaviness within her that she could not explain. She was deeply disappointed, though she had no idea why, at the viscount's easy surrender. She almost felt betrayed.

Chapter Nine

Accompanied by Dracourt and leaning heavily on his walking stick, Lord Edward hobbled down the garden path. Lingering pain accompanied his movements, but his frown was not caused by physical distress.

"Need to speak to you, Drax," he told his tall companion. "Personal matter."

"We'd best sit down first. You're not so steady on your pins yet." Dracourt led the way to a stone bench nearby. "What's bothering you, Ned?"

Lord Edward eased himself down on the bench and commenced chewing on his lower lip. He looked about him somewhat desperately. "Fine day," he said at last.

"So it is." Lord Edward relapsed into agitated silence. "The daffodils look uncommonly fine," Dracourt continued helpfully.

"Hang the daffodils," his lordship exploded. "You know very well—mean to say—" He made a superhuman effort and managed, "Drax, you cannot mean to offer for Daphne Larrimer."

Dracourt did not reply.

"Heard the commotion in the drawing room the other day. Couldn't help overhearing, don't you know. There I was in the morning room, and you were next door. And later there was that luncheon—God," Lord Edward continued fervently, "preserve me from another meal like that. Much rather face enemy fire, give you my word! My lady was looking like a cat that's swallowed the cream pot, the young bantam was glowering black murder, Rosalys Larrimer was as pale as a ghost. And her sister—" Lord Edward swallowed convulsively. "Drax, Daphne Larrimer was near tears. She does not want you to offer for her."

"The general idea," Dracourt said dryly, "is that the Larrimer relations are converging on Dorset in little more than a se'ennight. The engagement is to be announced then."

"You sound as if you like the idea!"

There was no humor in Dracourt's laugh. "Ned, I am so far from *liking* the idea that I've thrown my scruples to the winds. I actually tried to steal Kedwell's promissory note from Lady Larrimer."

"S-steal the note, Drax?" Lord Edward ran agitated hands through his hair spoiling the modish arrangement. "Oh, my God. But—but how did you know where the note was kept?"

"Angus told me. He said that my lady kept her important papers in a strongbox in her chamber. She wears the key to it around her neck."

Lord Edward's eyes were at the popping point. "Could not get the key then, I should think. I mean to say, dashed awkward place for her to keep it. What did you do?"

"I was going to try and force the strongbox. I got as far as my lady's chamber. I was almost inside. Then—"

"Your conscience smote you," Lord Edward said gloomily.

"Conscience be damned. I met Miss Rosa Larrimer in the hallway. I'll tell you, I was hard put to explain why I should be walking into her mother's chamber."

"Deucedly awkward," Lord Edward sympathized. "So it came to nothing?"

"Nothing," Dracourt agreed grimly.

A lark sang merrily close by, and the daffodils tossed their golden heads. The two men sat in such dismal silence that a robin, mistaking them for garden statues, ventured to peck at Lord Edward's Hessians.

His lordship shooed the encroaching bird away. "Have to make a clean breast of it. You do not love Daphne Larrimer, Drax. I—I—love her very much. Knew that was poaching on your preserves—could not help myself. Confound it all, she is an Incomparable, and—*oh, my God!*"

Dracourt turned to stare at his friend. "Are you in pain?" he exclaimed anxiously. "I thought it was too soon to come out-of-doors."

"Drax, why not offer for her sister?" Lord Edward demanded.

"I beg your pardon?" The viscount's voice was suddenly cold.

"You do not have a tendre for Daphne Larrimer," Lord Edward babbled. "I do. Never could hide anything from you. Never could hide my feelings at all, come to that. My nurse used to always know when I'd pinched an extra jam tart for tea. And Wiggins—you remember, our head gardener at Padgett Hall?—that man always knew when I'd run through his rubbishy flower gardens. All fun and gig, you know, but you'd think I'd committed highway robbery the way that brute cried rope on me! Many's the time my father gave me ten of the best because of Wiggins, blast him."

"Will you get to the point?" Dracourt gritted.

"Merely pointing out, dear old boy, that I love Daphne Larrimer. I've never felt this way for any female before, give you my word. I want to offer for her and can't, blast it. Shows a serious lack of feeling, proposing to your friend's fiancée."

The viscount seemed about to speak but apparently thought better of it.

"And now with old Lady Larrimer having this confounded house party and announcing your engagement—what I mean is," Lord Edward concluded, "why don't you offer for Rosa Larrimer? Kedwell's note doesn't specify which daughter. One sister would do as well as the other."

Abruptly, Dracourt rose to his feet. "Will you be all right alone for a while, Ned?" he asked. "Gallant's waiting for his morning ride."

Lord Edward detained him. "But what about my idea? Surely, it will answer if you offer for Miss Rosa?"

"No, it would *not* serve."

Undaunted by the viscount's icy tones, his lordship persisted. "Well, I'd like to know why not. You have to marry one of them. Kedwell's note—"

In a few savagely descriptive words, Dracourt described what Lord Edward could do with Kedwell's promissory note. Then he strode off toward the stables. Lord Edward stared after him. "What has got into that fellow?" he wanted to know.

A hail interrupted him, and he looked up to see a familiar curricle drive up to the gate. Tom Grady, now a regular fixture at Larrimer House, hurried to open the portals, and Windwoode guided his grays into the courtyard, threw the reins to Tom, and alighted. After pausing a moment to allow the world to admire his great coat with many capes, his waistcoat in that shade of pink called "the maiden's blush," and the fine points of his collar, he strolled over to Lord Edward.

"Feeling the thing this morning, dear boy?" he drawled.

"No," said his lordship with a frown. "Not feeling the thing at all. Where the deuce are you going, all prinked up?"

Windwoode buffed the nails of one hand on his sleeve and eyed them appreciatively. "There's a cockfight in the neighborhood. It'll do the young bantling good to see some sport."

At this moment Jeremy hurried from the house. He had obviously spent some time with his toilette, and his hair had been carefully arranged in the popular windswept style. He had been hard at work with his cravat, too, and had achieved a credible imitation of a waterfall.

"I'm sorry to have made you wait, Windwoode," he said eagerly. "Hulloa, Lord Edward. 'Pon rep, I'm glad to see that you're taking the air. Hope you are feeling the thing this morning?"

He did not wait for his lordship's answer but walked quickly to his fashionable friend's curricle. Lord Edward remarked that the boy now swaggered as affectedly as did Windwoode.

The sight left a bad taste. The Honorable Aubrey Windwoode, Lord Edward thought as he watched the two drive away, had seemed well enough when first encountered at Lady Bellingwane's crush in London, but the man did not *wear* well. And it was obvious that Drax disliked him. A good judge of character, Dracourt, and a true friend, though for the life of him he, Edward, could not understand why the big man had flown up into the boughs just now. It was unlike Drax to come all cold and toplofty because of a very sensible suggestion. After all, Dracourt had gone so far as to think of turning burglar to get at Kedwell's cockle-brained letter.

"Hang it, is there no way out of this coil?" Lord Edward asked himself. "I do not like it, give you my word. No, not above half."

*   *   *

"I do not like this. No, I do *not* like this above half."

Rosalys spoke to herself as she watched Windwoode's curricle draw up in the courtyard that evening. It did not sit well with her that Jeremy had brought his bosom-bow home for dinner—again.

Through the thick windowpanes of the drawing room, she could hear Windwoode joking about her brother's handling of his curricle. In the past few weeks Windwoode had taught him to drive. If that were all Jeremy had learned, she would have no cause to complain. But there were other things . . .

There was the studied insolence toward Dracourt, for one thing, and the distinctive Windwoode drawl that the younger man aped. There was talk of gaming with Windwoode's purse-plump friends. And this very morning Jeremy had been in a twitter of excitement about a cockfight, "which Windwoode tells me is quite provincial, but never mind. It is the first I have watched," he had bubbled.

Rosalys had on several occasions tried to speak to her brother about her concerns and had received a cold stare and the assertion that he was tired of petticoat government. Well, he may have reason. If only he could have chosen a better mentor. Lord Edward, perhaps, or—

She did not think the sentence through. She found it hard to think of Dracourt and to admit that the change in their relationship disturbed her. Until Lady Larrimer had forced the issue, there had been a warmth between them, a friendship. Now, she missed that friendship.

Rosalys missed talking to Dracourt. She missed his common sense and his humor. She had come to confide in the viscount, and now a wall had sprung up between them.

She did not know what to do about that wall.

Outwardly, Dracourt was preoccupied with helping Lord Edward along his road to recovery, exercising Gallant, or riding with Colonel Montfort. All this kept him busy. And when they met over meals or by chance, he was always pleasant and courteous to her.

Nothing had changed and everything had changed. Rosalys knew the barrier was there.

There was a difference in the way he looked at her, and the smile in his blue eyes that had always been there for her was gone. Of course, with Lady Larrimer forcing him into marriage, he could not be expected to feel any friendliness toward the Larrimers, but Rosalys wished that it could have been otherwise.

For one thing, she could have used his counsel. She had her hands full these days. Since her mother had informed her about her coming betrothal, Daphne had lapsed into a gloom so profound that not even the thought of the coming house party cheered her. Angus was having an attack of arthritis and was out of sorts, so with the exception of Lady Larrimer, and Cook, who continued to praise the Lord for her nephew's conversion, the household was a gloomy one.

Dinner that evening proved how true this was. Lord Edward was silent and morose. Daphne, in her sea green taffeta and lace, was red-eyed. Dracourt kept his own counsel. Only Jeremy, who was full of the cockfight he had seen, kept the conversation going.

His talk was so full of gore, however, that finally Rosalys protested. "I think that is enough, Jeremy," she said. "The mutilation of birds is hardly dinner conversation."

"It is a sport, ma'am," Windwoode protested.

"I must confess I never cared for such bloodthirsty diversions. The birds fight 'til one of them is killed, don't they?"

Windwoode raised his quizzing glass as if to examine an interesting species of bug and Jeremy exclaimed, "If that ain't just like a female. Who cares how a *fowl* dies?"

"Surely," Windwoode drawled, "the excellent capon we have just eaten did not die a natural death?"

He snickered and Jeremy laughed. Rosalys checked the angry retort that rose to her lips. There was no need to make matters worse by breaking straws at the dinner table. But as she fell silent, she heard Dracourt say, "Cockfighting is no favorite sport of mine, either."

"As it's the sport of *gentlemen*," Windwoode sneered, "that is understandable."

Even Jeremy looked a little shocked at this rudeness. Rosalys's eyes flew to Dracourt's face, but the big man only asked Jeremy, "How many cockfights have you seen before this?"

Jeremy glanced somewhat uncertainly at his
mentor, then back to the viscount. "None," he
blustered. "Windwoode says—"

"I say that the lad needs to learn what life is
about, Dracourt," Windwoode interrupted.

He was checked by a level stare. "With *you* as
teacher?" Dracourt demanded. "Only those who
are wise themselves should undertake that task,
Windwoode."

"And I suppose you're one of the wise men,"
the fop sneered.

"I know my limitations. That is the difference
between us," Dracourt replied calmly.

Windwoode bit his lip, and Lady Larrimer
rather hastily guided the talk into other channels.
"Her grace, your mother, has written to me,
Dracourt, saying that she cannot attend your betrothal. It is most regrettable, since I had wished
to make the dowager duchess known to all my
family." She paused and added triumphantly,
They will all be present. Even my third cousin
the Bishop of Constann will be here. And the
Marchioness of Lakefield has written me to say
that she will be present."

Daphne choked on oysters in escallop and had
to be beaten on the back. She then precipitously
left the table. Lord Edward gazed after her with
pitiful look.

"Nothing but tears and sulks here tonight,"
Rosalys heard Windwoode mutter to Jeremy.
"Give them the slip, bantling, and come with me.
Hanley and a few of our friends are setting up the

tables tonight. Just the thing to be rid of the blue devils, eh?"

Rosalys alomost protested then, and later she had to bite her tongue as she listened to Jeremy making his excuses to his mother. She wished that her ladyship would prevent him from leaving Larrimer House in Windwoode's company, but Lady Larrimer had other things on her mind. "Let the boy go," she said. "It must be dull for him after Oxford, and he and Dracourt do not rub along well. I do not want any brangling before the betrothal is formally announced, Rosalys."

Later, while the viscount and Lord Edward enjoyed their port and cigars, she asked her older daughter to accompany her to the morning room to discuss details of the house party.

"It has occurred to me that since all the guests —except for the Dowager Duchess of Kedwell— are coming, we will need servants," Lady Larrimer said. "Angus is poorly, and in any case cannot do all himself."

Rosalys agreed. "Poor Angus. He does his best, and it is hard to see him in such pain. I have already asked Cook to see if she knows some respectable women who will help us for a few days."

"That is not what I meant. We need trained chambermaids, and footmen," Lady Larrimer said. "Many members of the family will bring their own abigails and valets with them, but it will not look the thing if we are understaffed."

She paused and added, "And we must have music, as well."

"Why not?" Rosalys exclaimed. "I collect we may as well be hanged for a sheep as for a lamb."

Her mother ignored this. "We will need something to lighten the atmosphere. We cannot hold a rout or a crush—*that* would be unthinkable so soon after we have taken off the blacks for your dear papa—but a small orchestra will do very well. There will be some dancing. It is going to be a joyful occasion, after all."

Rosalys thought of Daphne's woebegone face and was silent.

"I know that all of this will *cost,*" Lady Larrimer continued, "but we must make a good showing. Depend upon it, all of them—especially my Aunt Lakefield—think that we have no feathers to fly with. They are curious about our reduced circumstances. How satisfying it will be to show them they are wrong."

"And *how* will we do that, ma'am?" Rosalys asked. Her mother told her. "Oh, Mama," she then sighed, "how can you say that this is a joyful occasion? It is sad. So very sad."

For a moment, the redoubtable Lady Larrimer looked like a sad old woman. Then, she rallied. "Fiddlesticks. If you have nothing to do but look Friday-faced, Rosa, go up to my chamber and bring me down paper and pen. I will write a note to that orchestra that used to play for us when your papa was alive. It is the beginning of the season, so they may not yet be engaged on that date."

Silently, Rosalys went upstairs. Her thoughts were far afield as she approached her mother's room, and it was not until she was close at hand that she realized that voices were coming from the chamber.

"Oh, it is no use," Daphne was saying bitterly. "We will never get the horrid thing open."

Rosalys peered through the half-open door and saw Daphne and Lord Edward trying to pry open Lady Larrimer's strongbox.

"What on *earth?*" She gasped.

The culprits jumped guiltily and turned to face her. They began to speak at once. "It was my idea," Daphne cried, and Lord Edward exclaimed, "Nothing of the kind—my fault completely."

Rosalys stepped into the room, shut the door behind her, and leaned against it. "Are you two *burglarizing* Mama's strongbox?" she demanded.

Lord Edward turned beet red and began to stammer explanations, but Daphne was defiant. "Yes!" she cried, "we wanted to destroy that horrid letter. We thought that you and Mama were engaged in planning that odious house party and that we would have time to do so." She placed a small hand on Lord Edward's arm adding, "Edward is here only because I begged him to help me."

His lordship would have none of this. "Beg you will not believe a word, Miss Larrimer," he said sternly. "I am the culprit. I mean—dash it—learned where Kedwell's letter was—took matters into my own hands. Reprehensible act for a gen-

tleman—but your sister's happiness means more
to me than my honor, don't you know."

"But we could not get the strongbox open,"
Daphne sighed. "Rosa, you'll say nothing to
Mama?"

Rosalys shook her head. "I almost wish you
had succeeded."

"There is nothing more to be done," Daphne
said despairingly. Her amethyst eyes looked even
more beautiful behind a veil of tears. "I must be
sacrificed so that my family can be saved. How
hard it is to go so young into the dark!"

Lord Edward put his arm around Daphne's
waist and led her tenderly from the room.
Rosalys was sure that his lordship didn't realize
that Daphne's touching words had been lifted
from a play they had once seen at Ashley's Am-
phitheater.

Even at such a time she could not help smiling,
and she found herself wishing that Dracourt were
there to share the joke. Suddenly, she could *feel*
him near her, hear his deep chuckle. For a moment warmth enfolded her, and then she shook
herself back to a reality where there *was* no
warmth. Silently she collected pen and paper and
went downstairs to her mother.

She remained with Lady Larrimer until past
eleven. The gentlemen had already retired, and
Cook was long abed. Rosalys oversaw the closing
of the house, forbade Angus to wait up for Jeremy, then sat and waited for him herself.

She could not sleep, anyway, and as the hours
passed and Jeremy did not return home, she be-

came more restless. After attempting unsuccessfully to read several books, she left her chamber and began to walk through the sleeping house.

Perhaps because of all that had happened that night, she was very aware of the age of the house. She remembered hearing of an ancestor who had ridden with Richard the First and another who had left wife and child to turn privateer for Elizabeth Tudor. There had been one Larrimer who had stood for Lancaster and another who had died for York.

These ancestors seemed to crowd around her as she walked down the wide staircase to the first floor, and they seemed to insist that Larrimer House must never be sold.

"But," Rosalys told the imagined crew, "it is not fair to Daphne and her Edward. They have the right to be happy, don't they?"

The ancestors expressed their scorn. Love and happiness must not be weighed against centuries of tradition. "Besides, you are not thinking of Lord Edward and Daphne," they sneered. "You are thinking of—"

"Damn you, Dracourt!"

Jeremy's angry voice, distant but quite clear, jolted Rosalys from her reverie. She stood listening intently until she realized that a murmur of voices was coming from the back of the house. Then, hastening to the servants' door, she caught up Cook's cloak and slipped outside.

The moon was nearly full but dimmed by wind-tossed clouds. That same brisk breeze carried Jeremy's words. "Confound you," he was protesting, "what right have you to rub your nose in my affairs? 'Pon rep, it's the outside of enough."

Dracourt's deep voice replied, but she could not make out what he said. "Jeremy, where are you?" Rosalys called.

A disgusted exclamation answered her, and her brother's slender form emerged from the bushes that grew around the back gate.

"Is everyone marching about tonight?" he wanted to know. " 'Pon rep, you and Dracourt might as well be the watch. You should be long abed, Rosa. It's past two."

Rosalys saw Dracourt standing some distance apart and thought she could guess what had caused *him* to walk out-of-doors at such a time. "Why were you creeping through the back gate?" she asked her brother.

"I wasn't *creeping*. I didn't want to wake anyone, did I?"

"Do not try and cut a wheedle with me, Jeremy," she was beginning, when her brother interrupted.

"What are *you* doing up so late, Dracourt? I say —you two aren't having a tryst?"

Dracourt ignored this. "You haven't told us why you were coming in the back gate," he pointed out.

Jeremy did not reply. "There is something very smoky going on," Rosalys exclaimed. "I want you to tell me what it is. No whiskers, please," she added sternly, as her brother began to speak. "Where were you this night?"

"At a party," he replied sulkily. "Ask Windwoode. 'Pon rep, Rosa, why are you blasting me like this?"

"You were gaming with Mr. Windwoode. I suppose you lost."

He had the grace to look shamefaced. "I didn't play for much, Rosa," he said. Then, stripling pride made him add, "I'm a man, hang it all."

Rosalys had to clench her hands so as not to box his ears. Then she uttered an exclamation of dismay instead. The moon had come out from its cloud coverings and shone full force on the gash on Jeremy's cheek.

"You are hurt," she cried, but he avoided her touch and fended off her anxious questions.

"It's nothing. If you must know, brambles are thick around the back gate, and one of them scratched me. That's all."

"Then why come that way?"

"I had the urge to walk there tonight." His sudden grin made him look years younger as he added, "Don't you remember how we used to hide-and-go-seek back there? I was thinking about those days, that's all."

There was a wistfulness in his dark eyes that caught at Rosalys's heart. Jeremy put an arm around her.

"The good times will come back," he told her huskily. "I know I have been not much help, but I swear I am trying to—I will help put things to rights, Rosa, see if I don't."

Then, as though ashamed of his display of feeling, he dropped his arm and strode away from her toward the house. Troubled, she watched him go.

Jeremy deserved a chance to enjoy life, she told herself. Daphne's marriage was not only going to save Larrimer House but Jeremy's future, too. Rosalys made herself believe that the sacrifice would not be too great. After all, Dracourt would be kind to Daphne, and he would eventually appreciate her charm and beauty. As for Daphne, once she had a fine house and clothes and jewels and servants to wait on her every whim, she might forget Lord Edward.

Surely, surely, Mama knew best. "It will be all right," she murmured aloud.

"I hope so."

So quiet had Dracourt been that she had forgotten he stood near her in the shadows. His words tumbled down the careful lies with which she had reassured herself.

"No," she sighed, "it will not come to rights. It is all wrong."

"Jeremy's gaming, you mean? It's something all boys his age pass through."

"No, I did not mean Jeremy. At least, he is a part of it, but—" She had not meant to tell him this, but the words came without her volition. "Mama is selling her tiara," she whispered.

Looking down into her unhappy face, Dracourt held himself in check. He must *not* speak, he reminded himself sternly. Not now.

"The diamonds in that tiara have been in the family for years and years, Connor. Mama is selling it to pay for the house party. To impress the family, especially our odious Grandaunt Lakefield." Too distressed to realize she had called him by name, Rosalys repeated, "It's all wrong. If you had seen her face tonight—"

She realized what she was saying and to whom, and checked herself. "I am sorry. None of this is your concern," she told him.

"But it *is* my concern. Damn and blast Kedwell's promise," Dracourt gritted. "Rosalys, I must tell you—"

But she was shaking her head. "No need to tell me. I know that you will soon be my brother-in-law through no fault of yours. I cannot blame you for wishing us all in Jericho." She attempted a smile. "I'm sorry, Connor, for enacting a Cheltenham tragedy."

There was a silence. It grew between them and spread like night shadows.

"It is very late," she said at last. "That odious boy was in the right about one thing. I should be asleep."

He escorted her back to the house where he bade her a toneless good night. Left alone, Rosalys felt suddenly exhausted, but even though she went to bed at once, she could not fall asleep, and when at last she did, her dreams were troubled.

She woke later than usual, and coming downstairs found Daphne and Jeremy breakfasting. Or rather, Daphne was playing with her boiled egg while Jeremy, his mouth stuffed with eggs and kidneys, was giving her advice.

"I know you do not want to be hobbled to

Dracourt, Daffy, but things might sort themselves out, you know. 'Pon rep, you may not have
to marry him after all.''

"What Banbury story are you weaving?"
Rosalys demanded, then frowned anew at the
deep scratch on her brother's cheek. She would
have liked to examine it more closely, but he
pushed her hand away.

"Take a damper, Rosa, and let me be. You females are always so—hulloa, what's that?''

There was a flurry of hoofbeats outside, and
unfamiliar voices rose from the courtyard. A moment later, Angus, bones creaking more than
usual, tottered into the room.

"There are persons who desire to speak to her
ladyship,'' he announced.

"Mama is yet abed,'' Rosalys protested. "What
do they want, Angus?''

The old man's face screwed up in disapproval.
"It is some person called Merchum, ma'am. With
him are two others under his command.''

"What the devil does he want?'' Jeremy
wanted to know.

"Merchum is a riding officer, sir. A exciseman.''

Jeremy stopped in the act of taking more kidneys and eggs. Rosalys, who remembered the little man she had seen outside the Royal George,
had a horrible thought. "Where is Tom Grady?''
she cried.

The sight of Tom Grady being dragged, kicking
and screaming, from Larrimer House would
throw Cook into spasms from which she might
never recover.

"He is not here, ma'am," Angus reassured her. "He did not come to the house this morning."

"Then why has the riding officer come here? No—never mind. I will speak to him myself." Rosalys turned to her brother. "I wish you will come too, Jeremy."

She did not see the reluctance with which the youth rose to his feet, for she had already passed through the hall and was descending the stairs toward the side entryway. There three men waited.

They wore nondescript woolen coats and dark hats, which they doffed when they saw her, the little riding officer with the rest. "Servant, ma'am," Merchum said. "Sorry to bother you so early, Miss Larrimer. I would like to see her ladyship if I may be so bold."

"My mother is resting, Mr. Merchum," Rosalys said courteously. "How may we aid you?"

She was aware of the little man's keen appraisal. "I am in Dorset on special orders from the Board of Customs, ma'am. It's to do with the smuggling that has been going on in these parts. The tidesmen have been in league with local revenue officials long enough, and London wants that practice stopped, see?"

"But how does this affect us? Surely you do not look for smugglers at Larrimer House."

To her surprise, Merchum nodded. "In a manner of speaking, ma'am, yes, I do. Begging your pardon, we tracked a suspicious character to these very gates last night."

"Of all the brass-faced lies!"

Cook had come onto the scene. Her large bosom heaved, and her eyes flashed with outrage. " 'Oo do you think you are, coming 'ere with your haccusations?" she demanded.

Dismayed, Rosalys ordered, "Cook, go back to the kitchen."

"Aye, heed your mistress, my good woman." Merchum's superiority made Cook puff up like a large and angry pigeon. "Be warned," he added unctuously, "that you can be charged with obstructing the law."

"Spare your breath to cool your porridge, you!" Cook snapped. "The law, is it? Then the law 'ad better go find somefink to do besides worry honest folks."

Merchum sucked his teeth. "Where was your nephew last night past one?" he demanded.

Cook did not hesitate. " 'E was wi' me. We was polishing the brass, there being a lot of brass to polish, what with the 'ouse party coming and all." She turned to Rosalys. "You know how it is, ma'am. Tom 'as been working 'ard lately."

This much was true, so Rosalys nodded. Merchum looked unconvinced. "Did *you* see Tom Grady here, ma'am?" he asked.

Rosalys met his probing gaze coolly. "If Cook says he was here, then he was here."

"Did anyone *see* the lad?" Merchum insisted. "Perhaps the young gentleman?"

Jeremy yawned in a bored way. "Past one, you said? Lord, no. If you people are cakes enough to go to bed at one in the morning, I am not. I was fast asleep at that hour."

"So you were abed that hour, sir?"

"Yes, I was," Jeremy replied coolly.

A horrible suspicion had begun to form in Rosalys's mind. She tried to dismiss it by telling herself that it was impossible, but as Merchum asked more questions, her disquiet grew.

At last the riding officer was done. He said that he was sorry to have taken their time, and as he went away with his men, Rosalys saw him glance once again at her brother.

"Well, if that ain't a Banbury story," Jeremy exclaimed disgustedly. "Smugglers—in Larrimer House! Did you ever hear such a maggoty notion?"

"Lord have mercy on us." Now that the riding officer had gone, Cook had become quite pale. " 'E were after Tom," she whispered. "An' I thought that lad were done with it an' all. Now that Merchum'll nab 'im."

"He's not going to 'nab' anyone," Jeremy reassured her. "No need to worry. Don't you agree, Rosa?"

But Rosalys was staring hard at her brother. He had just lied to an officer of the crown. But *why* had he lied?

"What's amiss now?" Jeremy asked. He gave a very credible imitation of Woodwinde's drawl as he added, " 'Pon rep, Rosa, why are you giving me that basilisk stare?"

She shook her head. "It is nothing."

Nothing of which I can be sure, anyway.

Chapter Ten

Though the Dowager Duchess Kedwell could not grace the Dowager Lady Larrimer's house party, Yorkshire was represented. Dracourt's valet, Pliskin, arrived some days before the gathering. A middle-aged individual, dapper from the top of his carefully combed black head to the soles of his immaculate boots, he appeared in a chaise crowded with portmanteaus.

"Her grace sends her greetings, may Lord," he intoned. "I have stayed away this while at your express command, but with the coming of your betrothal it was felt that my services might be of some small value."

With this, Pliskin proceeded to take over Larrimer House. He awed the newly hired staff, took ascendency over Lord Edward's valet, Vraewick, as was his due, and acted in so competent a way that he gained Angus's respect. Even Lady Larrimer approved of Pliskin, allowing that if the valet had come with his master from the start, Dracourt could never have carried off his role as country bumpkin.

This disguise had long since been discarded. Dracourt, attended by the urbane Pliskin, was in every detail the aristocrat. Daphne, deeply in love with her Edward, paid no heed to this transformation, but Jeremy eyed the tall peer with a certain awe. Rosalys also noted that her brother's cravats were no longer being tortured à la Wind-

woode but tied with the elegant simplicity that
the viscount favored.

A change for the better—but then, everything
was changed these days. A very different spirit
pervaded Larrimer House as preparations were
made for Daphne's betrothal.

Angus had the overseeing of a trio of new footmen and a brace of chambermaids, and was looking harried but important. Cook, at first disposed
to resent the London caterers hired for the occasion, realized that they were old retainers from
Sir Henry's heyday and was cheered by the fact
that the caterers were so eager for the patronage
of the future Viscountess Dracourt that they did
not even mention the horrible word "payment."

Lady Larrimer was in her element these days.
She criticized, complained, and chivvied the
newly hired staff unmercifully, sending one footman into such a quake that he was heard to mutter that he must have been a tiddlepoop to have
taken a place with such a stiff-rumped mistress as
his lady.

As usual, the complaints came around to
Rosalys. "For it's feathers one day an' fowl the
next, if you get my meaning," Cook told her
young mistress on the long-awaited day of the
house party. "I can't say what 'er ladyship is
thinking, Miss Rosa, ordering seven and eight
dishes a course for the dinner tonight. There's
money today, but it won't last 'til tomorrow if
you gets my meaning."

Rosalys privately agreed with her but said
aloud, "This is the first time we are entertaining

since Papa died. We must all put our best foot forward."

She reminded herself of this good advice as the morning produced their first guest. The Marchioness of Lakefield arrived quite early, traveling in a stately coach that was followed immediately by a humbler vehicle bearing her abigail and maid-servant, luggage, and two footmen.

Bringing up the rear of this procession came the duchess's youngest son, Marnay. Marnay fancied himself a Corinthian and a nonpareil, though Jeremy later confided to Rosalys that his horses were a pair of bone-setters. Blissfully unaware of this fact, Marnay handled his bays with as much pride as he wore his fashionable garments.

Rosalys watched all this from the drawing room window. "Indeed, if Cousin Marnay is not in the tweak of fashion," she exclaimed. "Come and look, Daffy. If his shoulders of his coat had higher peaks, we wouldn't be able to see his head."

She spoke cheerfully to distract her drooping sister. The ploy did not work. "Grandaunt Lakefield looks more disagreeable than usual," Daphne sighed. "Oh, why did she have to be our first guest?"

As a person of consequence, the marchioness expected a formal welcome. All three ladies went downstairs to greet her at the door. Here Rosalys and Daphne curtsied deeply while their mother offered her cheek to her aunt.

"You are looking very well, ma'am," Lady Larrimer said.

The marchioness smiled. She had a small mouth, and the smile did not alter its disagreeable lines. Her black eyes were also small and gimlet-keen, and her long nose seemed fairly to quiver with curiosity.

"You are looking quite the thing, Gratiana," the marchioness said in the whispery voice that always made her sound as though she were rehearsing for her deathbed. "Country living must agree with you. You have put on meat since I last saw you. And here are your gels."

Realizing that those sharp black eyes were surveying her critically, Rosalys curtsied. "You are looking very fine, Rosa. I collect that age does not alter a woman very much *unless* she is a beauty." The marchioness turned her mean little smile on Daphne. "And yes, Daphne—do not be put out, my child. When you are the Viscountess Dracourt, I am sure you will be able to afford gowns that are much more the thing."

Daphne bit her lip. Rosalys, battling both annoyance and laughter, turned to her cousin and inquired about the trip. Marnay tried to answer but was upstaged by his mother.

"We were obliged to lay at Bridesbridge the night. Inns are so uncomfortable, Gratiana. I told my host this morning," the marchioness sighed, "that since his food was unpalatable, his servants incapable, and the beds uncomfortable, I would withhold something from the bill."

Lady Larrimer and Rosalys exchanged a speaking look. "Will you come upstairs and remove your pelisse, Aunt?" her ladyship invited. "Though, of course, you know the way well in Larrimer House."

"It has been a long time since I was here." Black eyes searched for dust in the hallway, unerringly honed onto the worn spots in the carpet. "A *very* long time," the marchioness whispered triumphantly.

Marnay offered Daphne his arm as they followed the two ladies. Rosalys turned with a wry smile to Angus, who was standing by. "She is sure to discover the darns in the sheets. Can you imagine what she will say to us tomorrow?"

She had little time to refine on this, for other guests now began to arrive. First came the Scottish cousins and their three unmarried daughters. Next appeared Lady Strafton, the late Sir Henry's sister, her son Percy, and her second husband, Mr. Gerard Mannering, who was rumored to be a fortune hunter. Following them came His Grace the Archbishop escorting the ancient Mrs. Bushing, his late wife's aunt. This lady was rather deaf and very crotchety and complained loudly that the Yellow Room in which she was installed was not up to snuff at all.

Other relatives appeared in their turn. Satisfying everyone and making sure that their servants were properly billeted kept Rosalys busy all morning. Nor did luncheon allow her any time to rest. Many of the guests were fatigued, so trays had to be sent up to their rooms. Moreover, because Daphne did not appear and Lady Larrimer was resting for the night's activities, Rosalys presided over the table and watched her grandaunt try to goad Dracourt into anger.

In this the marchioness was unsuccessful. The viscount remained peaceful. After trying some of her more vituperative barbs, Marchioness Lakefield turned to the morose and uncooperative Lord Edward. Being frustrated on two fronts, she then targeted Jeremy. Rosalys tried to intercede at this point—Jeremy loathed his grandaunt and was not shy about saying so—but to her surprise he parried the marchioness's barbs with good humor.

In fact, he was in excellent spirits. Considering the fact that he loathed Daphne's coming marriage, Rosalys wondered what possessed her younger brother. Perhaps he had become reconciled to it all, she thought, as she watched him talking animatedly.

The marchioness sniffed. "Jeremy has a feverish look," she said. "Putrid throat is much about these days, so it *may* only be that."

Rosalys glanced at her brother's heightened color and was suddenly anxious. "Do you think so, ma'am?"

"I do indeed." said her grandaunt pleasantly. "Naturally, he is sickening."

Rosalys caught Dracourt's sympathetic eye. She looked quickly away, but little escaped the marchioness.

"I collect that it is strange," she said in her most carrying whisper, "that your sister should not be with us at luncheon. But since her betrothed has been looking at *you* all this time, we must trust that he does not pine for her."

"You are roasting me, ma'am," Rosalys said quickly. This was mistake. Seeing that a victim had at last presented herself, the marchioness whetted her tongue.

"I beg you will not refine upon it too much. Men, after all, will look at any eligible female. He is not yet married, and you are, of course, a spinster."

Others were listening, and Mrs. Bushing was loudly demanding to know what was going on. Rosalys felt her cheeks flush with annoyance, but she held her peace. Any remonstrance would only encourage the odious woman.

"It is such a shame," sighed the marchioness, "that you are buried in the country, my dear. No one sees you here. Even *if* you had the beauty to attract a suitor—but a respectable older man may present himself. Yes, indeed, I would imagine him to be a widower. With grown children, of course."

"Let me wish you happy, ma'am!"

Voices around the table hushed and those persons already listening craned forward interestedly as Dracourt got to his feet. He reached across the table, clasped Lady Lakefield's hand, and pumped it enthusiastically. "The single state is a sorry one, so it's much better to marry. You're wise, ma'am."

For once, the marchioness was silenced. Her mouth popped open, and her small eyes glazed a little. Seeing this, Jeremy jumped into the breach.

"I wish you happy also, ma'am," he crowed. "A widower, I think you said your suitor was?"

"Are you quite mad?" the marchioness sputtered. "I did not mean that *I* was to marry anyone. And let go of my hand immediately, sir!"

Dracourt left off shaking the marchioness's hand. "I'm sorry. I forgot that older ladies are prone to rheumatics," he apologized.

Machioness Lakefield rose abruptly, said something disparaging about the food, and swept from the room. Jeremy immediately went into whoops of laughter.

"Your trick, Dracourt. 'Pon rep, that was neatly done. I never thought that old gorgon could be silenced—oh, I beg your pardon, Marnay."

But the marchioness's son was grinning widely. "You do not have to beg *my* pardon. I never saw such a lovely sight as Mama's face just now." He raised his wineglass. "Cousin Connor, I salute you. Welcome to the family."

Dracourt looked at Rosalys and smiled. "I misunderstood what was going on, that's all."

The smile was his old smile. The warm look was back in his eyes. Rosalys felt as if something that had gone cold and hard within her was stirring back to life. When he looked at her in that way, it was as if—

Mrs. Bushing banged the table and demanded to be told what everyone was laughing about. Rosalys had to placate the old lady, and when she next glanced at Dracourt, he was talking to Lord Edward as if nothing had happened.

The newfound warmth within her died. The

blood stopped coursing through her veins in madcap abandon.

Gudgeon, she told herself. Nothing did happen!

"It is just like the old days," Daphne said. "The lights and the flowers and—Rosa, I wish I were dead."

Rosalys's heart ached for her sister, but she said cheerfully, "Fudge, Daffy, you are looking much too beautiful to wish yourself dead."

Though certain that heartbreak prevented her from living another moment, Daphne could not resist peeping into her mirror. She did look exquisite in pale amethyst sarcanet. Carefully, she smoothed the blue satin underskirt of the first new dress she had had in two years.

"I would be the happiest girl in the world if it were Edward to whom I was becoming engaged," she admitted.

"Do you dislike Connor so excessively?" A trace of wistfulness had crept into Rosalys's voice. "Truly, it was too bad of him to pretend to be a country cousin, but you know he is nothing of the kind."

"I know that I have nothing against him, Rosa, truly. But I don't want to marry him, and he does not care tuppence for me. I think he has a tendre for you."

"Fiddle," Rosalys exclaimed.

"Oh, Rosa, I wish Mama had never found Kedwell's letter."

For one moment Rosalys allowed herself to

think of what might have happened if there were
no letter. Then she squared her slender shoulders.
"You must not show a weepy face in front of our
guests," she said. "Smile, Daffy."

As Daphne had pointed out, the house had
been transformed. Candles gleamed in sconces on
the walls, their costly scent mingling with those
of hothouse flowers. On the first floor, across
from the drawing room, the great hall had been
scrubbed and polished and prepared for dancing.
Chairs had been set for the guests, and the orchestra was playing softly.

As Rosalys and Daphne descended, they saw
Lord Edward at the foot of the stairs. He wore an
expression of such anguish that Rosalys's heart
ached for him.

So intent was she on her sister's troubles that
she did not note the man who stood in the shadows beside the great hall. Dracourt, watching
both the women, was thinking that he didn't
blame his friend for losing his heart. Daphne had
never looked so dazzling. In her rich new gown,
she was like a princess out of a fairytale.

Even so, his eyes were drawn to her older sister. Rosalys carried herself with an unconscious
charm, an ineffable grace that owed nothing to
the neat but uninspired orange-blossom crepe
gown she wore. Since her face was turned toward
Daphne, Dracourt could see only her profile, but
—what long dark eyelashes she had, he thought,
and when she smiled encouragingly at her sister,
the curve of her lips invited kissing. If she would
look his way—

Drawn by some force she could not explain, Rosalys turned her eyes toward the great hall and thought she saw a stranger. Dracourt had dressed for his betrothal in severe black and white. A single diamond glinted in the impeccably tied cravat. His fair hair gleamed, and he held himself proudly. Connor St. Cyr, Viscount Dracourt, had never looked so handsome.

Nor had he looked so grim. Rosalys glanced at her sister's mournful face and felt her heart sink. But before despair could take hold, Lady Larrimer came sailing out of the great hall.

"Ah, Rosalys, Daphne. Come into the hall— they are all waiting. Because of Mrs. Bushing and the bishop, we must keep country hours tonight, I fear. It is so odious to eat at six o'clock, but old people must be humored, so we will announce the betrothal after we dine." She looked keenly at the two silent men before adding, "Do you not think Daphne looks particularly charming tonight, Lord Dracourt? Pray take her in at once. And you, Lord Edward, be so good as to escort Rosalys, if you please."

Daphne barely touched the arm of her unsmiling escort. Rosalys felt Lord Edward's whole body quiver as they followed the soon-to-be betrothed pair. "Are you in pain?" she whispered. "No one would blame you if you were forced to go and lie down."

He squeezed her hand in silent thanks. "Cannot fight shy," he told her. "Have to face the fire like a man, don't you know."

She herself felt cowardly as they entered the

drawing room. So many people were there. There were the relations, of course, and old friends like the Montforts. All of these people were gazing curiously at Dracourt and Daphne, and she could see the speculation in the marchioness's malicious eyes.

It was a relief when Angus announced dinner and Dracourt took Daphne in. They made an elegant pair and were seated near the head of the table. Rosalys, placed between the bishop and Lord Edward, tried to follow His Grace's discourse on ancient relics of the Faith. Meanwhile, she kept glancing at Jeremy.

It concerned her that her brother displayed the same feverish gaiety he had shown during luncheon. He looked excited and cheerful. *Why* was the wretched boy so cheerful? But perhaps it was a defense, his way of trying to get through the horrible evening.

And it *was* horrible. The family, en masse, was enough to overwhelm anyone. So was the sumptuous dinner. Used to plain fare, Rosalys hardly tasted the multitude of dishes before her.

She was grateful when the ladies left the gentlemen to their port, though her relief was short-lived. Determined to revenge herself for her earlier humiliation, the marchioness poured die-away venom into her grandniece's ear. *What* could Catherine Strafton have been thinking of marrying that mushroom, Mannering? Mrs. Bushing was near senile, and you could tell that the bishop had an eye to her fortune. And was not Larrimer House falling to ruin? Surely this marriage to the plump-pursed Dracourt had come in the nick of time. How sad it was that it would probably be an unhappy one.

Knowing that argument would only encourage the wicked old lady, Rosalys bit her tongue. It was near to bleeding by the time they rejoined the men in the great hall, and she was grateful that the dancing gave her an excuse to leave the marchioness's side.

The first dance was a cotillion. Dracourt stood up with Daphne, and Rosalys searched the room for Jeremy so that he could partner her, but she could not find him. He had probably slipped out after dinner to spend the rest of the evening with his bosom-bow, Windwoode—and for once, Rosalys did not blame him. She wished she could escape herself.

She danced the cotillion with her cousin Marnay. As he led her back to her seat, Dracourt returned with Daphne. Rosalys noted that her sister looked even more miserable than before. "My fault," Dracourt apologized. "I trod on Miss Larrimer's foot as we danced."

"Pray do not regard it," Daphne said faintly.

A country set had begun to form, and Dracourt smiled and held out a hand. "Will you try again, ma'am?"

Daphne paled and looked imploringly at Lord Edward, who had taken a nearby seat. "Are—are you more familiar with country dances, sir?" she asked hopefully.

"Hardly. Soldiering does not leave time for the most elegant pursuits," Dracourt explained. "But there is no time like the present to learn. With a charming partner I may overcome my clumsiness."

Daphne looked trapped. "My sister is such an excellent dancer, Lord Dracourt. She could teach you far better than I could." Amethyst eyes pleaded with Rosalys, *Help me, Rosa!*

Lord Edward added, "Good idea. Can not dance with one lady all evening, Drax, bad ton, don't you know."

"Well, Miss Larrimer? Are you courageous enough to dance with me?"

There was a glint of mischief in his eyes. Glad that he seemed to have shaken off his earlier grim mood, Rosalys rose to her feet and let him lead her to her place. But when the set had begun, she realized what she had done. Dracourt was a horrible dancer.

"I can't get the hang of it somehow," he confessed. "Mincing about a dance floor is something my feet aren't trained to do. Besides, it's stifling in here. I'd give a great deal for a draught of cool air."

Rosalys followed his gaze to the tall french windows at the end of the great hall. "It would be rag-mannered to leave the others," she murmured longingly.

"No one need see us." Cleverly, Dracourt edged his partner toward the windows and then whisked them both outside. "There, isn't that better?"

She had to admit that he was right. After the stuffiness inside the great hall, the cool April air was bracing. She breathed it gratefully and listened as the orchestra struck up a waltz.

"Do you waltz?" he asked.

"I expect you will now ask me to teach you how," she sighed.

"Well, will you?"

Before she could agree, he had slid an arm around her waist and drawn her close. Then, moving with a swift and sure grace, he swirled her into the garden.

After a few moments she stopped dancing and drew away from him. His closeness, the muted music, and the darkness had left her oddly breathless. "When will you stop telling whiskers?" she demanded sternly. "To pretend that you could not dance!"

"It all depends on my partner, Rosalys."

"That is another whisker. And—and you are impertinent, sir."

His eyes shone silver in the moonlight. "I told you what to expect if you called me 'sir' again."

He put his arms around her and bent his head to hers. Her head tipped back, and her mouth rose to meet his. Their lips met. Passionate, needful lips took hers and held them hostage. Under his insistent mouth her lips trembled open.

Waves of fire seemed to curl through her. They awakened feelings she couldn't recognize. A muted inner voice warned that she must stop this madness, but she could not break his embrace. What she wanted was to go on being kissed like this forever.

"Rosalys," Dracourt murmured. "I love you."

I love you, the night seemed to sigh.

"I want to marry you," Dracourt then said.

Reality surged back like a black tide. A hand seemed to close tightly about her heart. "It is not necessary to pretend," she managed to say.

He drew back from her a little. "What do you mean by that?"

"That you need not lie. I—I know that you are offering for me so that Lord Edward can marry Daphne."

He frowned. "You think I'm doing this for *Ned?*"

"He is your friend."

He swore savagely. This was so uncharacteristic that she stared up at him in astonishment. "Do you think I am sacrificing myself? Before God, Rosalys, I was afraid of this. That is why I waited so long. But there is not time left, my love, and I must—"

There was an apologetic cough from the shadows. "May lord," Pliskin's voice said.

Rosalys took several steps backward. Dracourt swore again. "What the devil do you want?"

"I regret, may lord, that there is something that will not wait." Pliskin seemed his unflappable self, but there was an undercurrent of tension in his voice. "I beg that your lordship will follow me. And you, too, ma'am, if you will be so kind. It is of the utmost importance."

Dracourts fine mouth tightened. "The young cub?"

"Yes, may lord."

"Do you mean Jeremy?" Rosalys cried. "Oh, I

knew that something was afoot. Has anything happened to him?"

A trace of agitation surfaced in Pliskin's voice. "I beg you to come this way."

They followed him around the house and to the servants' entrance. "The caterers are in the kitchen and may see you, so we must wait until the cook can distract them," Pliskin explained. There was the sound of breaking dishes and Cook's loud accusations. "Now, please, may lord and madam," Pliskin breathed.

They hurriedly bypassed the kitchen and stepped into the servants' quarters. There, Angus stood guard at the door of his room. When he saw Rosalys, he uttered an exclamation of relief. "Thank God you have come, Miss Rosa. He will not listen to me."

Dracourt pushed past the old man into the room. Rosalys, who followed close on his heels, covered her mouth with her hand to push back a cry of horror. Jeremy was lying on bloodstained sheets on Angus's narrow bed. His coat and waistcoat were off, his shirt was open, and blood seeped from a wound in his chest. Seeing Rosalys and Dracourt, he tried to rise.

Rosalys ran to the bedside. "Do not move. We must get a doctor. Angus—"

"No." Jeremy grasped her hand with a frighteningly weak clasp. "No doctor," he panted.

Dracourt bent over the wounded youth. "The wound is too low for the heart or lung. Rosalys," he ordered, "I need hot water. Hand me a clean sheet, Angus."

Angus was already tearing a sheet into strips. As Rosalys sped from the room, Dracourt wadded the sheeting and held it tight against the wound. "You've lost a lot of blood," he went on sternly, "but you aren't about to die. Believe me, I've seen men fight an entire battle with more hurt than this. Still, the bullet's lodged in you, so a doctor must be called."

"I will go now for Dr. Whittiwell, sir," Angus offered.

"No!" Jeremy almost screamed. "Listen to me—"

"I know what you're going to say," Dracourt interrupted grimly. "You've become embroiled with the smugglers."

As he spoke, Rosalys returned to the room with the hot water. It took all her self-control not to tip the bowl. "Smugglers," she breathed. "How could you do such a mad thing?"

Her brother gave her a disgusted look. "Ain't that exactly what a hen-witted female'd say?" he demanded. "Of course I did it because I didn't want Daphne to marry Dracourt."

"I do not see any 'of course' about it," Rosalys shot back. "And who are you calling hen-witted? How could smugglers stop Daphne's marriage?"

Jeremy turned to Dracourt. "*You* understand, don't you, Dracourt?"

Dracourt, engaged in washing the wound and staunching the by now sluggish flow of blood, said crisply, "You felt that if you could get your hands on enough blunt, you could pay off your father's creditors and so make my marriage to Daphne unnecessary."

Jeremy had the grace to look embarrassed. "Nothing against you," he mumbled. "Only Daffy don't want to be nobbled to you."

Dracourt finished his work in silence. "This is a stopgap measure," Rosalys said urgently. "The doctor has to be called."

"Humgudgeon, Rosa, you don't understand anything," Jeremy declared. "I can't stay here much less wait on a sawbones. Merchum suspects I was mixed in with this night's work."

Pliskin explained, "I believe that the officers of the law are hot on young Master Jeremy's trail, ma'am. Like bloodhounds after a fox, so to speak."

Dracourt ordered him to stow the poetic imagery and to see whether Merchum was anywhere about. Pliskin glided away.

"They're about all right," Jeremy groaned. "It was cursed bad luck. We knew that that riding officer was on to us. We were going to try one last haul. Tom said—"

"Tom Grady," Rosalys said bitterly. "Of course he would be at the bottom of this sorry business. No wonder he was so obliging as to come and work at Larrimer House. That made it convenient for the two of you to make your maggoty plots."

"I wish you would not interrupt a fellow so," her brother complained. "Anyway, Tom said that the coast was clear. He was lookout. But he ran for it without warning me, and Merchum's man winged me. Tom got away, of course, and so did the others."

His words trailed off as Pliskin returned to the room.

"How many?" Dracourt demanded.

"Four, may lord. The riding officer, two underlings, and—there is another."

Rosalys saw a look pass between the valet and his master. Meanwhile, Jeremy struggled to a sitting position. "They're bound to catch me. I don't know how they knew it was me. Disguised. No one knew except—" He paused.

"Except Windwoode." Dracourt's mouth was set in a harsh line. "You told him about the smugglers, didn't you?"

"Well, I did," Jeremy said defensively. "Windwoode thought it was a grand joke." He paused. "Are you saying that he'd squeak beef on me? Because if you are—"

"It does not signify who told the excisemen," Rosalys interrupted. "They must not find you here. Jeremy, you must go away."

"Master Jeremy cannot travel, ma'am," Angus quavered.

Rosalys raised hands to her aching forehead. Angus was right. Jeremy could never outrun the law. And if they found him here, wounded—

"I'm leaving," Jeremy panted. "No, Dracourt, I will get up. I will, I say. I must ride farther on. Can't let those damned excisemen learn I took shelter here—"

"Lie down, you young fool. And the rest of you, listen to me." Dracourt's voice cracked with authority. "If Jeremy is apprehended as a smuggler, it may mean prison. Certainly it will mean disgrace." He let this sink in and then turned to the old butler. "Angus, go out and greet Merchum and his men. Be appropriately outraged that they have dared to come to Larrimer House at this hour. Can you carry it off?"

The old man drew himself to his full, frail height. His Scottish burr reverberated like war drums. "I have ser-rved the family for many years, my lord, and I have never yet failed in my duties."

"Good. And, Angus, on your way send Cook in with a bottle of spirits. Now, Rosalys—"

He checked himself as he met her dark eyes. She had bravely put aside her fear and was now ready to obey his orders. "Don't look so worried, sweetheart," he said softly. "We're not finished yet." In a louder voice he added, "You must return to the party. Tell your mother that I've acted in a disgusting way. Make her believe it." *Leave it to me,* his eyes told her.

Rosalys left the room quickly. Warring with her anxiety over Jeremy was something else that made it hard for her to think. She knew that Dracourt had only offered for her because of Kedwell's promise. And yet just now, he had called her sweetheart in a way that brought an ache to her heart.

She couldn't understand any of it. Neither could she understand herself.

Chapter Eleven

The marchioness's malicious little eyes had taken due note of her niece's absence. As Rosalys returned to the hall, she saw her grandaunt whispering in Lady Larrimer's ear.

Remembering that she had a part to play, Rosalys threaded her way through the dancers to her mother's side.

"Where have you been?" Lady Larrimer demanded.

"And where," the marchioness added significantly, "is Lord Dracourt?"

It was easy to look mortified. "I am sure that I do not know, ma'am."

"Do not cut a wheedle with me," her mother said sternly. "Your grandaunt saw you and Dracourt leave together. It is time to announce the betrothal, and he is not here. Where is he, pray?"

The Marchioness of Lakefield's long nose quivered. "You have been having a cose with your sister's affianced bridegroom?" she suggested.

Rosalys thought of Jeremy lying wounded. Real tears filled her eyes. "Oh, it is too odious for words," she exclaimed.

Lady Larrimer looked alarmed. "Rosa, what has happened between you and Dracourt?"

"It is obvious that the loose screw has made an attempt on the gel's honor." Rosalys's grandaunt was enjoying herself hugely. "He threw sheep's eyes at her all through luncheon, and it was as plain as a pikestaff that the libertine had base intentions. If you were not such a wet-goose, Gratiana, you would have seen it for yourself."

"No, you are wrong. That is not what happened." Improvising freely, Rosalys sank into the chair next to her suddenly pale mother. "It is too, too hideous for words, Mama. He . . ."

"He . . . ? Well, *what* did the loose fish do, Rosa?"

Not quite sure what Dracourt was supposed to have done, Rosalys was grateful to see Angus coming toward them.

"Some persons insist on speaking with your ladyship," the butler announced.

"They *insist?* Who, pray?"

Angus looked down his twisted beak of nose. He exuded so much disdain that Rosalys wanted to applaud. "They are, I regret to say, persons of the law. A riding officer, my lady, by the name of Lieutenant Merchum. And his underlings."

"Riding officer?" Lady Larrimer was so aggravated that her small frame seemed to swell. "Really, what the world is coming to I cannot tell you. Decent people cannot be free of intrusion from these jumped-up excisemen." She gestured imperiously. "Inform this Meeham that I shall see him in the morning, Angus."

"I took the liberty of doing so already, my lady. He said that his business was pressing and that if your ladyship did not go out to him, he would come in to you."

Lady Larrimer made a sound between a gasp

and a gobble. The marchioness looked radiant as she solicitously patted her niece's shoulder.

"Calm yourself, my dear. Perhaps you had best go out and see what the fellow wants, after all. It would not be seemly to have him appear among the family."

This horrible thought had evidently occurred to Lady Larrimer. With an outraged rustle, she rose to her feet. "Where is Jeremy? As a mere female, I would have wished for his company." She looked about the great hall. "Do you know where *he* has gone to, Rosalys?"

"I'm sorry, Mama, but I do not."

"No matter. I shall deal with this Meehen myself. Remain where you are, Aunt, I beg. This matter is soon disposed of. Rosalys, come with me."

Rosalys followed with her mother out of the great hall and down the stairs toward the side entrance. There in the entryway she could see four men. There was Merchum, the two men who had accompanied him that other morning, and Aubrey Windwoode.

The riding officer and his followers were in drab uniform. In contrast, the Honorable Aubrey Windwoode blazed like a comet. He was arrayed in a long-tailed coat of spring green, a waistcoat of the same color, and striped green pantaloons. His neck cloth was tied in the Mathematical style and featured a large emerald. A long cloak lined in green silk hung from his shoulders.

Windwoode had outdone himself, but even more striking than his clothing was his expression. Noting the look on the man's pudgy face, Rosalys remembered Dracourt's stern question and Jeremy's defensive answer. "So it *was* he," she murmured.

Seeing Windwoode, Lady Larrimer turned to him gratefully. "Mr. Windwoode," she exclaimed. "I am glad to see you. I beg that you will stay and listen to these *persons.*" She turned majestically to Merchum. "I take it that there is some reason for this intrusion?"

Merchum coughed against his fist. "I regret it very much, your ladyship, but we have reason to believe that a fugitive's taken refuge in your home."

Lady Larrimer's eyelids narrowed, but she remained ominously silent. "And what leads you to this idiotic notion, sir?" Rosalys demanded.

Merchum sucked his teeth. "He was followed here," he said, "from his place of ran-dey-voo with the other smugglers."

"Smugglers? Is the fellow mad, or in his cups, Rosalys? I have no knowledge of tidesmen. No one here does." Lady Larrimer gathered her skirts with one small hand, and gestured imperiously with the other. "Show these gentlemen the door, Angus."

"Wait." There was a triumphant note in Aubrey Windwoode's drawl. "You may not know about smuggling, ma'am," he continued gloatingly, "but your son does."

"My *son?*"

Her ladyship's tone could have caused stone blocks to crumble. Even Merchum started.

"Do you mean to tell me," Lady Larrimer continued in the same voice, "that you accuse *my son* of being involved with smugglers? That is malicious slander, sir. You are attempting to blacken an old and honorable name. I am a mere female and cannot call you out, but I tell you to your teeth that you are a liar,"

"And a villain," Rosalys added feelingly. All her dislike for Windwoode throbbed in her low voice.

"Calling me names will not alter the fact that your brother's involved with smugglers. He told me so."

Rosalys's hands itched to fasten themselves around Windwoode's hateful throat. "Jeremy is your friend. How can you speak so of him?"

"You're not so high in the instep now, are you?" he mocked her. "You laughed at me before this, you and your precious viscount. 'Pon rep, now I am the one who laughs." His expression changed to the vicious hatred she had seen before as he added, "We'll see how 'old' and 'honorable' your name is when Jeremy is transported for his crimes against the Crown."

He was doing this for spite. It was a craven's mean and cowardly revenge. "You should be horsewhipped!" Rosalys cried.

Merchum said, "Gently, ma'am. No use fatching yourself. We're not here to cause anyone trouble but to see the young gentleman. I have a few questions for him."

He got no further, for at this moment raucous singing could be heard in the near distance. It broke off, dissolved into male laughter, then began again.

"What, in the name of God, is that?" Lady Larrimer demanded.

The side door banged open and in staggered two very drunk gentlemen. For a moment they stood swaying in the doorway, then the foolish grins on their faces dissolved into expressions of comical dismay.

"M-mama," Jeremy stammered. He raised a weak hand, waved, and dropped it to his side. "Hullo, Mama."

Rosalys bit her lower lip to stop from crying out. Bright spots burned on Jeremy's cheeks, but otherwise the lad was very pale. His hair was disheveled, his eyes wild. He leaned heavily on Dracourt, whose great arm was clamped about his shoulders.

"I told you, lad," Dracourt groaned. "Didn't I, now? 'Let's go by the back way,' I said. Now, did I say that or didn't I?"

Jeremy hiccuped. "My house," he said with dignity. "Your house soon, Dracourt. Man shou— man should be able to walk through his own door anytime he wants to."

"Good heavens," Lady Larrimer said faintly.

"Give you good morning ma'am," Dracourt crowed.

"Not mornin' yet, Dracourt," Jeremy protested. "Bad ton, wishing people good mornin' when it's evening." He seemed to find this statement hilarious, for he repeated it several times.

Rosalys caught Dracourt's blue eye. It met hers

steadily, then lowered slightly in a wink. Taking her cue, she rounded on him.

"Lord Dracourt," she said indignantly, "this is too shabby of you. Did I not tell you that your behavior was contemptible? And to get Jeremy foxed as well—oh, it's the outside of enough. And as for you, you detestable boy, I could box your ears!"

Jeremy started to giggle. He leaned against Dracourt's shoulder. "Females don't understand, do they?" he said.

Dracourt glanced blearily at Rosalys, and lurched toward her. A smell of strong spirits moved with him. "You both stink of the taproom, sir!" she cried.

Dracourt lifted an arm and sniffed his coat sleeve. "Don't smell anything. Had a li'l drink with my future brother-in-law, here. One little drink—"

"Two li'l drinks," Jeremy corrected gravely. "Three. Four l'il drinks. Where's the bottle, Dracourt? I'm thirsty."

"Young chub's bosky," Dracourt explained. "I told him to stop—told him several times this night. He wouldn't."

Rosalys glanced at Merchum and his men. They were staring with their mouths half-open. "You see how it is, Mama," she exclaimed tragically.

She was grateful to note understanding dawn in her ladyship's eyes. Lady Larrimer might not know Dracourt's plan, but she was no fool.

"I am persuaded that you encouraged my son

in his excess," she berated Dracourt. "For shame. You, a guest in my house. You are a base creature, sir."

"Oh, I say," Jeremy hiccuped. "Doing it too brown, Mama."

His voice was more than ever slurred, and Rosalys was terrified that at any second he would fall down in a faint. He looked so pale and wan, and his limbs, for all his gallant efforts, were shaking. She knew that he was only standing through force of will and because Dracourt was supporting him.

"Cockle-brained young scamp," she scolded. "You will be sick in a moment. Go to bed at once."

But Merchum objected to this. "Not so fast, please. Where have you been this evening, young sir?"

"Me?" Jeremy demanded. He turned to Dracourt. "That fellow referring to me?"

Dracourt squinted at the riding officer. "I think he is."

"Don't know what he wants. Do you know what he wants, Dracourt?"

"Where," repeated Merchum grimly, "were you this evening? There, I have said it plain and cannot say it plainer." He took a step toward Jeremy, but Rosalys stepped between them. "Move aside, miss," he commanded.

"I will do no such thing. My brother is foxed and is going straight to bed. You can ask him questions in the morning if you must."

"If he does not answer my questions now, I

will arrest him," Merchum threatened. As he
spoke, there was a stir on the first floor. The
doors of the great hall opened to disgorge Lord
Edward and Daphne, who hung on his arm.
Rosalys's heart sank to see that the tall and avidly
curious figure of the Marchioness of Lakefield
glided behind them.

"No need to take that tone, my man," Jeremy
said. "Ladies present. Where was I? Drinking, of
course. Along with Dracourt, here."

"All evening?" the riding officer asked ominously.

"Oh, off and on, you know. Dra-Dracourt
couldn't get away. Had to dance with my sister,"
Jeremy supplied helpfully. "Poor fellow's gotten
caught in parson's mousetrap."

The newcomers had by now descended to the
side entryway. Lord Edward looked about him,
correctly summed up the situation, and put
Daphne gently aside.

"Drax, told you it was shabby," he lectured.
"Told you not to get Jeremy disguised." He
turned to Merchum, adding coolly, "I am Lord
Edward Padgett, former captain in the third
dragoons. I wish to state that I have nothing to do
with this disgraceful affair. Nothing."

"What disgraceful affair, sir?" Merchum asked.

"Boozing, of course. These sap-skulls wanted
me to join them. They have been swilling off and
on, all night. Or rather, Jeremy was swilling and
Drax stole off whenever he could. No wonder
they are bosky."

"But," Daphne began, "he did not seem—"

"Of course the viscount was foxed." Rosalys
swiftly interrupted. "That is why he stamped on
your toes so often, Daffy. He stepped on mine,
too, I can assure you. It really is inexcusable. On
his betrothal night, too!"

The marchioness's little eyes gleamed. "I must
say," she said in her die-away voice, "that Dracourt's behavior does not surprise me. Put any
man within ten miles of a bottle, and he will be
drunk. As for Jeremy, his behavior has been extraordinary all day. I daresay he has been drinking since the afternoon."

Merchum was losing ground and knew it. Two
peers of the realm had vouched for the suspected
smuggler's whereabouts. He looked sharply at
Windwoode, who was yet another blood of the
ton. "This gentleman is sure that young Master
Jeremy is involved in smuggling," he began.

Contempt shouted from every line of Lord Edward's suddenly hard face. "Oh—you believed
him, did you?"

Windwoode winced, but exclaimed, "Hold on
a moment. 'Pon rep, I know what I know. The
bantling told me he was involved with the
tidesmen."

Ignoring Windwoode, Lord Edward spoke to
Merchum. "If you are such a gudgeon as to believe what *Windwoode* tells you—but then, you
would not know," he added generously. "Man's
noted for it. Lies all the time. Probably lies in his
sleep."

Windwoode tried to protest, but his words
were drowned out as Daphne burst into tears.

"And to think," she wailed, "that I nearly was betrothed to this—to this drunken creature! To this libertine!"

"Now you've done it," Lord Edward groaned. "Drax, why did you have to go and shoot the cat on this night of all nights? Think of what the poor lady is suffering."

"Not as much as I suffered, being forced to dance and mince around like a lady's maid," Dracourt protested. "I looked like a proper fool tripping this way and that." He took a few unsteady dance steps and collapsed, along with Jeremy, onto a sofa that stood near the doorway. Silently, Rosalys blessed him. Jeremy couldn't have stood up for very much longer.

"They are lying, all of them," Windwoode hissed. "Merchum, do your duty!"

The harassed riding officer turned an unfriendly eye on Windwoode. "I can see my duty without your help," he snapped.

"But surely it's plain that the boy's lying," Windwoode snarled. "He's no drunker than I am. If you'd just do your duty instead of listening to a lot of nonsense—"

Merchum closed his eyes, drew a deep breath, and shouted, "Shut up, sir!"

There was silence. The riding officer glared around him. "There is a lot going on that's smoky, and I am going to find out the truth to all this. And the first thing that I do is to arrest young Master Larrimer."

"You mean to stand there and tell me that you

intend to arrest my son?'' Lady Larrimer demanded.

Her ladyship's compelling tone had its effect. Merchum looked about him for support and saw that his two men were avoiding his glance. He then clapped his hand to his pocket where his orders were. Taking courage from them he pulled himself together. "Yes," he said, "I am."

Jeremy giggled. "For shooting the cat? Come on, inspector. You'd be arresting half the men in England."

"I am arresting you for being involved with the smugglers," shouted Merchum.

Rosalys turned agitated eyes toward the first floor, but the doors of the great hall remained closed. Inwardly, she blessed the fact that the side entrance was some distance away from the merrymakers and that the musicians were playing a loud and spirited cotillion.

"You're as queer as Dick's hatband if you think this young whelp had anything to do with any smugglers," Dracourt said. "Why," he added in a scornful voice, "he couldn't smuggle anything. Couldn't ride, neither, come to think of it. Tell you what," he said, struggling to his feet and lurching across the room, "he can't even hold his liquor."

He threw a confiding arm around Merchum's shoulders. The riding officer attempted to pull free but found himself rooted to the spot by the big man. "Young nincompoop," Dracourt confided, breathing boozy breath into the other man's face with every word. "Can't drink.

Shouldn't have got him started, but there you have it. Man don't get shackled every day."

The viscount hiccuped loudly. Jeremy, who had looked half-asleep, reared up at the sound. "Sir, you'll take back those words!" He attempted to stand but instead slid back onto the settee. "Take it back before I call you out," he slurred.

"But I've no reason to *go* out," Dracourt remonstrated.

"You know what I mean. You accused me of not being able to hold my liquor. I res-resen—I resent that and challenge you to a duel here and now," Jeremy insisted.

"A duel!" Rosalys grasped Merchum's arm. "Lieutenant, you must stop them."

The little riding officer struggled to free himself. "I am trying to," he said. "Lord, miss, if you would just—no one is fighting any duels here. By order of the Crown!"

"Oh, be easy. I wouldn't cross swords with a callow youth," Dracourt sneered.

"Callow youth! Well, hang it, that does it." Jeremy stared around the room until his gaze alighted on Lord Edward. "You'll act as my second?"

"You can't have Ned," Dracourt said promptly. "He's my friend, not yours."

"Highly irregular procedure," Lord Edward allowed. "No—what am I saying? Of course I will not be your second, young madcap, because you are not fighting anyone. You are a trifle scragged, don't you know."

Jeremy began to snap imprecations at Dracourt.

Under cover of this, Lord Edward drew Merchum aside. "If I were you, I would get myself and my men out of this," he advised. "If you leave, we will be able to calm them down. Your presence is goading them along in this lunatic behavior."

Not for the first time, Merchum looked uncertain. He hesitated.

Jeremy tried to heave himself to his feet, then collapsed again. "I need gloves. Who's got gloves? Can't call a man out without gloves."

"Do not lend him any gloves!" Rosalys wailed. "Nobody lend him any gloves!"

"Time to go," Lord Edward urged. "Bound to be a dust-up, shouldn't wonder. Family business. *You* know how it is."

Won by the confiding tone, the riding officer unbent a little. "Lord, yes, sir." He hesitated. "If you will vouch for the fact that these gentlemen *were* here all night—"

"Don't listen to him," Windwoode yelped. He added desperately, "Dracourt is covering up for the stripling, can't you see that? He's a future brother-in-law, ain't he?"

"Are you questioning my honor?"

The question cracked through sudden stillness. All eyes were immediately riveted on the tall figure of the viscount. He held his big frame erect, his blue eyes blazing in a suddenly stern face. His lips spat out the words as if they were bullets.

"Are—you—calling—me—a—liar?"

With none too certain a gait but with deadly intent, Dracourt strode across the room toward

Windwoode. The Honorable Mr. Windwoode ducked behind Merchum.

"I call on you to protect me," he cried. "Get away, Dracourt. I'm shielded by the law."

"Not anymore." Dracourt's arm shot out, caught Windwoode by the collar, and hauled him close. "In Spain," he said in the same deadly, deliberate voice, "the toreadors have a custom. They give the ears of a slain bull to the lady of their choice. I'm minded to pull your ears off and present them to my future bride."

Windwoode opened his mouth, but no sound emerged. Lord Edward now limped manfully forward. "Let be, Drax. He ain't worth it. Pathological liar—everyone knows it. Nobody who is anybody receives him. Ain't that right, Lady Lakefield?"

The marchioness, who had been tongue-tied until now, rose magnificently to the occasion. "Indeed," she said in her nasty whisper, "the name of—what is it again?—oh yes, Windwoode —is a hissing and an abomination in polite circles. Cut dead by the Marquis of Billingsgate in the park! Refused admittance at the Duchess of Parkmin's residence! Thrown out of White's!"

Windwoode attempted speech, but Dracourt's grip on his throat prevented him. The big man bent close. "I know that you cut those saddle cinches," he said very quietly. "I *know* you, Windwoode, clear down to your nasty soul. I'll give you until I count to three to remove yourself from my sight. If you are still here at that time, I'll call you out and kill you. Understand?"

He gave the fop a small shake and let him go. "Officer," Windwoode gurgled, "aren't you going to do something?"

Merchum turned away.

"One," said Dracourt.

"The man is lying," Windwoode bleated. "He's covering up for—"

"Two."

Windwoode turned and bolted for the door. He slipped as he reached the portals and nearly fell, but Angus obligingly held the door open and closed it behind the fleeing man's back.

"Three," said Dracourt with a smile.

Jeremy lapsed into drunken giggles. "Saw his face when he ran, didn't you? Really thought Dracourt was going to take his ears. Dunghill courage!"

Merchum pursed his lips. "All the same, sir," he began.

"Sirrah!"

Merchum blanched a little as Lady Larrimer advanced upon him.

"Lieutenant, do you know who I am?" her ladyship demanded. "I am the Dowager Lady Larrimer, widow of Sir Henry Larrimer. My father was the Marquis of Loring, and *his* father the Earl of Flaywraite." She paused to let all this genealogy trickle in. "How dare you suggest that any of my blood could be connected to a band of common smugglers?"

Each word she spoke crackled. Her eyes blazed with so cold a fury that Merchum could not meet them. "My authority is from the Board of Customs," he muttered.

"Your *authority* came from a despicable creature who has since left the scene," Lady Larrimer said coldly. "I beg to remind you that this is *my* house. You trespass upon us. You have dared to come and enact a Cheltenham tragedy here. You have dared," Lady Larrimer continued, warming to the task, "to annoy my guests. You have dared to inflict Windwoode's lies upon us."

Merchum pulled out a handkerchief and mopped his brow.

"That fellow still here?" Dracourt demanded. He glared at Merchum. "Are *you* calling me a liar? Ned, is he calling me a liar?"

"Lord Edward has stated that my son was drinking all night with this—*gentleman.*" Lady Larrimer practically sneered the word. "Is not Lord Edward's word good enough?"

"If any man says I'm a liar, I'll call him out," Dracourt insisted stubbornly. "Where's my sword?"

Rosalys caught Merchum's arm. "You see that he becomes unmanageable. Gentlemen in their cups often are. Please, sir, leave us."

Lord Edward nodded. "Best for all," he agreed. "Understand your position. Trying! To be lied to —and then having to witness this argle-bargle. Terrible what you riding officers go through. Brave fellows. Couldn't do it myself."

Dracourt was still demanding his sword. Jeremy had begun to once more call for gloves. Daphne had finally realized what was going on and was entreating her mother not to force her to marry Dracourt. The marchioness was joyfully embroidering on anecdotes that showed Windwoode's perfidy.

Merchum had never felt more uneasy. He had distrusted Windwoode from the start. A gentleman who would peach on another was despicable. He was sure, now, that jealousy and spite had made the wretched little fop tell lies.

He tried to gather the rags of his authority around him. "I'm sorry for this evening's work, and that's for sure. But that gentleman insisted—"

Lady Larrimer extended an imperious finger. "Go!" she commanded.

Merchum went silently. His minions trailed after him in hasty disorder. Angus, who was standing by the door, let them all out and closed the door behind them. There was the sound of footsteps, of hoofbeats, and then mercifully, of silence.

"Have they gone?" Daphne whispered.

Before anyone could answer, Jeremy sagged back. His eyes closed. Dracourt bent quickly down, picked up the boy, and carried him from the room. As Rosalys followed, she could hear her grandaunt demanding explanations.

"She will get more than explanation unless a surgeon is sent for," she cried in anguish.

Dracourt reassured her. "Don't worry. Pliskin went for the doctor. Now that Merchum and his men have gone, he'll bring the sawbones in. Ah, Pliskin," he added as his manservant, followed by Dr. Whittiwell, met them in Jeremy's room, "well done."

The valet bowed. "You will need hot water, may lord. I will fetch it. The less number of persons who know about this incident the better."

Pliskin disappeared downstairs, and Dracourt laid Jeremy on his bed. The boy tried to smile through bloodless lips.

"Hung on as long as I could," he gasped. "We bamboozled Merchum, didn't we, Rosa?"

"Famously. You should be on the stage."

She fell silent as Lady Larrimer swept in followed by her aunt, Daphne, and Lord Edward.

"Shut the door," Lady Larrimer commanded. "We want no more people in here." She looked at her aunt's avid countenance and her face worked. "We are in your debt, ma'am," she murmured.

"Say no more," that lady whispered. "I have not enjoyed myself as much in a year's time. That Windwoode looked to be a particularly nasty creature, and besides, family is family, and blood is thicker than water."

During this speech, Lady Larrimer had knelt down beside the bed. "Doctor, how does he do?" she asked. Assured that her son would live, she added, "I need not ask whether or not you were involved in that disgraceful affair. Jeremy, what I have to say to you will wait until you are stronger, but I am shocked. Shocked! Supposing Merchum comes back?"

Lord Edward shook his head. "I doubt it, ma'am. He'll know it was his word against ours."

Lady Larrimer considered this. "That is so. I am

obliged to you, Lord Edward. But had it not been
for Dracourt's quick thinking—"

"Be in the basket," Lord Edward finished
cheerfully. "All Drax's planning. Never was such
a fellow for thinking on his feet. Remember one
time on the Peninsula when we were surrounded
by Boney's men. Absolutely surrounded.
Thought we'd be cut down where we stood. But
Drax convinced the Frenchys that we were
drunken peasants until we were close enough to
engage." He nodded wisely. "Knew you were up
to something when I saw you pretending to be
drunk because you never get bosky, Drax. Emp-
tied a bottle of whiskey all over you and the boy,
didn't you? Thought so."

Lady Larrimer had been chewing her lower lip
during this monologue. Now she said, "We are in
your debt, Dracourt. If there is something I can
do to repay you, you have but to name it."

"Is that so?" Dracourt spoke coolly, but his
eyes sparkled like blue fire. "In that case, I beg
you'll tear up Kedwell's letter."

Chapter Twelve

"I cannot do that," the Dowager Lady Larrimer exclaimed. "You must not ask *that* of me."

"Your ladyship said that you would do anything within your power," Dracourt reminded her.

"Yes, but!"

Lord Edward cleared his throat. "I am witness to your words, ma'am. You gave your word."

He looked speakingly at Daphne, who silently clasped her hands and held them out to her mother. Lady Larrimer turned her back.

Rosalys went to her mother's side and put an arm around her shoulders. "Jeremy was foolish tonight because he was desperate for money, Mama. He wanted to stop the marriage at all costs. Except for Dracourt he would be on his way to Newgate at this moment."

Lady Larrimer shuddered. Then, moving jerkily, she put her hand to her neck and drew out a silken cord on which hung a key. She handed the key to Rosalys. "Go and get the letter," she said.

Rosalys sped to her mother's chamber and withdrew the letter from the strongbox. When she came back, Dr. Whittiwell was gone and so were the servants. Only the family remained grouped about the room: Lady Larrimer seated at Jeremy's bedside, Daphne and Lord Edward standing close together at the foot of the bed, the marchioness enthroned on a settee near the window.

Dracourt, arms folded across his chest, leaned back against the wall closest to the door. His eyes questioned Rosalys as she came through the door. She answered it indirectly by saying, "Here is Kedwell's letter, Mama."

Lady Larrimer took the letter. Her voice was toneless as she said, "Lord Dracourt, what I am about to do will spell the downfall of our house."

"Now who's making a Cheltenham tragedy?" Jeremy wondered.

Lady Larrimer ignored him. "Lord Dracourt, do you still insist?"

"Yes," Dracourt said.

Gray eyes and blue, equally implacable, met and locked for a long moment. Then with a gesture that was as grand as it was tragic Lady Larrimer tore the letter into two. "It is done," she sighed.

Daphne clapped her hands and skipped for joy. Then, catching Dracourt's smile, she blushed prettily. "I beg your pardon, my lord. Please, it is not that I dislike you, but we are not suited. I pray we may be friends."

Nothing could be more graceful—or as gracious —as the tall man's bow. "Your obedient servant, ma'am," he told her.

Lady Larrimer sniffed.

"Don't look so Friday-faced, Mama," protested her irrepressible son. "Of course it ain't the ruin of the house. Padgett's bound to offer for Daphne."

Lord Edward gamely stepped forward. "Lady

Larrimer," he cried, "beg your permission to pay my addresses to your daughter!"

"Humgudgeon," Jeremy pronounced scornfully. "As if he ain't been paying addresses all along. I saw them in the morning room once, and they—*ow!*" he yelped as Daphne reached out and pinched him. "I say, Rosa, I'm a wounded man. I need something to drink."

"All you will get is barley water," Rosalys warned.

She was glad for an excuse to leave the room. She felt caught between laughter and tears, and as she closed the door to Jeremy's chamber behind her, those foolish tears prickled against her eyelids. It was, she told herself, an idiotic thing to want to cry now that everything had worked out so well. Lord Edward's portion might not be as great as Dracourt's, but he would certainly not allow his wife's family to be evicted from Larrimer House. And as to Dracourt himself—

He was free. The sword that had dangled over his head had been taken away, the noose removed from about his neck. "I am glad," Rosalys told herself. Then she thought, only now he will go away, and felt an ache deep in her heart.

But she rallied almost immediately. Why should he stay? she demanded of herself. It was only natural that he would want to end this deplorable episode in his life. They could only be grateful that the viscount was too much of a gentleman to regale his friends with the adventure of Kedwell's letter. Now they all could continue with their lives.

Rosalys paused at the head of the stairs and
considered her own future. She knew she was going to be very busy helping her mother put the
house to rights. Lady Larrimer would no doubt
want to make costly repairs, but though Lord Edward would satisfy Sir Henry's creditors, he
could not be expected to pay the bills for Larrimer House's renewal. Economies must be made,
and, as usual, she would have to be buffer between reality and her ladyship's imperious will.
And then, there would be the wedding—

Rosalys smiled, imagining Daphne's wedding.
When Daphne married her Edward, they would
visit often. Eventually, they would bring their
children to Larrimer House. "That will be wonderful," Rosalys told herself happily.

"Are you talking to yourself?"

The familiar voice caught her by surprise. She
had not heard Dracourt come up behind her. Either he could walk like a cat, or the music from
the Great Hall had masked his footsteps.

"What is so wonderful?" he wanted to know.

"Daffy's wedding to her Edward," she explained. "It's possible now."

"All's well that ends well, Rosalys."

She ignored both his familiar use of her name
and the leap of her pulse. "But there is one immediate problem," she pointed out. "The family
downstairs must be faced. I'm more grateful than
I can say that the music kept them from hearing
us brangling, but when they hear about Jeremy's
disgraceful conduct—"

"Why should they have to hear anything?"

"Oh, come! Someone is sure to have noticed our absence."

He disagreed. "The news that Daphne is going to marry Ned instead of me will explain that. The marchioness will help smooth things over."

"Grandaunt *Lakefield?* Connor, I think that you are truly foxed. She will delight in telling everyone the details of what happened tonight."

Dracourt grinned. "No, she will not. She's going to tell everyone that Ned caused a rumpus by declaring his undying love for her grandniece. The marchioness will add that Lady Larrimer was reluctant at first, but that the young lovers' eloquence overcame her scruples. I, of course, magnanimously renounced my claim to Miss Larrimer in favor of my friend."

"Grandaunt is going to help us? *Why?*"

"Because, as she says, blood is stronger than water. She might enjoy raking coals over the family herself, but she will be damned if she will let outsiders do it. Besides, she had the time of her life ringing a peal over Windwoode."

Rosalys sighed. *"That* I believe. I hope you may be right about the rest."

"Depend on it." His blue eyes danced with laughter. "That muffin-faced wretch really believed that I would tear his ears off. He'll be raising dust on the road to London by now."

"Good riddance to him!" She paused. "What are your plans now?"

"I'll be leaving for Yorkshire," he said simply.

She ran her hand along the polished banister. "I see." Downstairs, there was a break in the music. As voices drifted up, she added resolutely, "I must go down."

"Wait, Rosalys."

Held back by the deep voice, she stopped with her foot on the topmost step. "We were having a conversation when Pliskin interrupted us," he reminded her.

"I—I had forgotten about that."

"Had you?"

Standing very straight, she faced him. His face was partly in shadow, but she could see the tender curve of his lips. "That conversation is not necessary now. Kedwell's letter has been destroyed."

He took hold of the hand that lay on the banister. She tried unsuccessfully to pull it away. "Is that what you think?" he was asking.

"What else? You *know* it is true." When he did not respond, she continued. "You waited until the last possible moment, hoping that something would change Mama's mind. Then, when your betrothal to Daphne seemed inescapable and you were quite beside the bridge, you offered for *me* so that you could free her—and Lord Edward. I understand, you see."

Her lips trembled into a smile. He said nothing but looked down into her upturned face. The new shadows in her eyes gave him confidence. "Do you, my love?" he asked.

"You are a man who is loyal to his friends, but there is no need to sacrifice yourself now. The letter is gone, and—*what* did you call me?"

"My love," he obliged her. "My dear love."

There was no warning. One moment, he was speaking in a perfectly normal way. Next second, Rosalys was caught and held in strong arms.

"What are you—"

But the "doing" was never uttered as the viscount stopped her lips with his. If she felt any need to protest this assault, it was not for long. Rosalys returned Dracourt's kisses with as much enthusiasm as they were given.

"I love you," he said after a long time.

"And I, Connor—"

He silenced her again. Their lips stayed together for many minutes. Only the need to breathe made them draw apart.

"I have loved you for so long. But Kedwell's letter kept me silent," Dracourt confessed. He was luxuriating in the feel of her in his arms, in the soft firmness of her lithe body, the intoxicating scent she wore. "I was afraid that if I told you how I felt, you would not believe me. I was sure you would feel as you did tonight—that I was offering for you for Ned's sake."

"Because you had to," she murmured against his cheek. "I could not bear that, Connor."

"Well, you will not have to. I can tell you now, without fear of being misunderstood, that I love you. And of course, you will marry me."

For answer she drew his head down to hers for another long kiss. Then, leaning in his arms, she rested her head against his broad shoulder. "I have wanted to do this for so long," she confessed blissfully.

He stroked her dark hair. "I meant it, you

know, when I told your mother I meant to offer for her daughter. Only, I meant I would offer for you. The trick was in finding the right moment to declare myself."

Before she could respond to this, the door to the great hall banged open and Mrs. Bushing's querulous voice could be heard.

"Where is Gratiana? Where is Rosalys and the viscount? Where is everyone? It is too bad of them to have deserted us."

"I collect that the time for explanations has come." Rosalys's smiling eyes met Dracourt's. "But before we explain about Lord Edward and Daphne, we should perhaps tell Mama about us. Connor, she will think you are humbugging her again. We had best tell her together."

He hugged her and then linked her arm through his. "Aye, lass," he said. "We must always be together from now on, thee and me."

Reading—
For The
Fun Of It

Ask a teacher to define the most important skill for success and inevitably she will reply, "the ability to read."

But millions of young people never acquire that skill for the simple reason that they've never discovered the pleasures books bring.

That's why there's RIF—Reading is Fundamental. The nation's largest reading motivation program, RIF works with community groups to get youngsters into books and reading. RIF makes it possible for young people to have books that interest them, books they can choose and keep. And RIF involves young people in activities that make them want to read—**for the fun of it.**

The more children read, the more they learn, and the more they **want** to learn.

There are children in your community—maybe in your own home—who need RIF. For more information, write to:

RIF
Dept. BK-3
Box 23444
Washington, D.C.
20026

Founded in 1966, RIF is a national, nonprofit organization with local projects run by volunteers in every state of the union.